SWEETHEART'S *Lake*

SWEETHEART'S *Lake*

SEAN KIKKERT

SWEETWATER BOOKS
An imprint of Cedar Fort, Inc.
Springville, Utah

ISBN 13: 978-1-4621-4262-0

Published by Sweetwater Books, an imprint of Cedar Fort, Inc.
2373 W. 700 S., Springville, UT 84663
Distributed by Cedar Fort, Inc., www.cedarfort.com

Library of Congress Control Number: 2022935673

Cover design by Shawnda T. Craig
Cover design © 2022 Cedar Fort, Inc.
Substantive by Rachel Hathcock
Edited and typeset by Valene Wood

Printed in the United States of America

10 9 8 7 6 5 4 3 2 1

Printed on acid-free paper

To my sweetheart and true love, Jaquilyn

Gratitude, dear wife, for making me believe in true love again, for being my best friend during the darkest time of my life, and for teaching me to enjoy the journey.

Chapter One

LONDON, ENGLAND. 1815

"Checkmate," Alicia Bartlett declared with an air of triumph as she brought her black queen down upon her brother's white bishop. As the ornate ivory chess piece toppled over onto the pretty rosewood board, Alicia brushed an unruly lock of fair hair away from her vivid green eyes. She was a tall, elegant-looking girl with a serious expression, and high cheekbones. She always wore her long, flaxen locks up and beneath a bonnet in public, but around the house she much preferred to allow it to tumble freely about her slender shoulders.

"I don't believe it," her brother, Oliver, declared with a sigh, "you have managed to beat me yet again, Alicia. How can that be possible—you're just my *little* sister!"

"I am nineteen years of age now, Oliver Matthew Bartlett, and you will be well served to remember that," Alicia teased with a fond smile. Alicia's dear brother, a little over four years her senior, had lorded his seniority over her for as long as she could remember. He always jokingly maintained he was their parents' favourite offspring, too, being the one and only male child in the Bartlett household.

Oliver Bartlett was a handsome young man, a stocky fellow with hair as black as Whitby jet and his father's distinctive, dark-brown eyes. He had always been the wild one of the two Bartlett children, with a proclivity for drinking in London's public houses and indulging in his favourite sport of boxing. Alicia, on the other hand, was shrewd and eager to learn. Even at the tender age of nineteen, she had a wise head upon her slender shoulders. Oliver had, thus far, exhibited very little desire in following in his father's footsteps of becoming a barrister; he much preferred the company of his questionable bunch of friends at Offley's sporting hotel down Henrietta Street or The Daffy Club in Holborn. His mother made no bones whatsoever about her disapproval of her son's pugilistic activities, even though his father was quietly proud and would live vicariously through his son's tall tales of nights of debauchery as they shared their occasional evening brandy and cigars. And, of course, being such a strikingly fine-looking young man, Oliver Bartlett had no shortage of female admirers—and thusly had no intentions of even pretending to look for a wife.

"Oliver, I do wish you would encourage your sister to engage in more ladylike pursuits," their mother said as she bustled into the drawing room. "Chess is a game for gentlemen, and gentlemen only."

"Perhaps, then, that is why I always beat Oliver." Alicia poked her tongue out at her brother, much to Mother's chagrin. Such boorish behaviour was precisely why she didn't encourage her offspring to associate too much—it didn't take too long at all for Oliver's mannerisms and attitudes to rub off on his sister. Mother was finding herself admonishing her daughter more and more often for unladylike language.

"And that is no way for you to behave, either, young lady," Mrs. Bartlett chided with a wry smile. Dorothea Bartlett was a tall, willowy, youthful-looking lady who carried herself with the correct feminine grace and poise befitting a genteel, upper-middle-class lady, yet had the rapier wit and acid tongue of a fishwife when provoked. The family lived in an imposing five-storey Georgian house in the affluent part of Bethnal Green, which Dorothea preferred to describe to friends as comfortable. She ruled that household with an iron fist and accepted little by means of nonsense from either her husband or children. "Put that away," she growled and pointed at the chess set. "Your father will be home from his work shortly, and heaven forbid he catches you playing it, my dear—you know how he can be with such matters."

Alicia knew all too well the antiquated attitude of her father, the renowned barrister, Dudley Bartlett Esquire. Should he have his way, he would have his sweet, chaste daughter doing nothing more than sitting by the fireside with embroidery while she awaited some eligible young bachelor to happen along to whisk her away. He father even considered the Jane Austen books Alicia so loved to be a terrible influence and had banned them outright from the house.

"Shouldn't Father be home by now?" Oliver asked as he carefully packed the chess pieces away, one by one, into their velvet-lined case. "I'm so hungry for dinner."

"When are you *not* hungry, Oliver?" Dorothea snapped at her son. "He will be home when he gets home—he had some sort of business to attend to at the club."

"He has an after-hours meeting with Edmund," Alicia told them both with a coy grin.

"I swear that young man is putting in more hours at the courts than most of the other barristers put together," Dorothea declared with a sigh. "Heaven only knows how he will cope once he's called to the bar—how will he ever find time for you, my dear Alicia?"

Alicia smiled at the thought of Edmund Pembroke, her beau and unequivocal love of her life since they were both in their teen years. Just three years older than she, Edmund was slim, quite perfectly tall, with mousey brown hair, a magnificent moustache that curled up at its edges and striking hazel eyes that sparkled bright with love whenever Alicia was in his presence. Edmund came from a family of similar social standing to the Bartletts and from a long line of barristers and lawmakers. Indeed, his great uncle Barnaby had once contended for the position of Member of Parliament for the rotten borough of Willerby-on-the-Marsh, which elevated the family still higher, especially in the Bartletts' eyes. But more than anything, Alicia's parents recognised Edmund as an unusually kind and pure soul who would cherish their daughter. All in all, young Edmund had more than earned Alicia's parents' consent to woo their precious daughter. As for Alicia, she was amazed how Edmund was able to see right through her. Sometimes she thought he knew her too well.

"I am confident that Edmund will find time for me once we are wed, Mother," Alicia said.

"And just when will that be, I wonder?" Dorothea replied with a huge, theatrical sigh. "He is forever busy, and you insist on partaking in terribly un-wifely pastimes—your pursuit of writing is downright unseemly. I fear I will be cold in my grave before I hear wedding bells for either of my children." The barbed comment was aimed more at Oliver, of course, who simply ignored it, as he did all the others.

"I guess it very much depends upon what Father has to say to him this very evening." Alicia stood up from her chair and smoothed down the front of her plain blue dress.

Dorothea opened her mouth as if to speak, but then the farthing dropped, and she put two and two together. "Edmund is asking for your hand?" With a broad smile spreading across her handsome face, Dorothea strode across the drawing room with her arms outstretched. "Why on earth didn't you say so, you silly girl?"

"And spoil the surprise for you?" Alicia laughed.

In a rare display of open affection, Dorothea gathered her dear daughter into her arms and hugged her so tightly she could barely breathe. "I am *so* delighted for you, my darling Alicia," she declared. "And here was I thinking you were so headstrong as to be destined to die a spinster—how fortunate we are that you have beauty in your favour."

"It looks like you have beaten me at this, too, dearest sister of mine." Oliver patiently waited his turn to congratulate Alicia. "I do suppose this lets me off the hook now, especially when you begin to churn out grandchildren for Mother and Father."

Alicia laughed at that and, as she extricated herself from her mother's embrace, she turned to her brother's silly, grinning face. "I feel you may be a little premature in your assumptions, Oliver," she told him. "Before you go planning children on my behalf, and before Mother heads off to Savile Row for wedding suits, do remember I have not been asked yet—nor is my reply a given. Providing Father gives Edmund his consent, I will still need to give the young man my answer."

Of course, everyone knew that was only a matter of formality, and Alicia was only trying to keep her mother and brother in suspense. Alicia had fallen profoundly in love with Edmund the moment she had set eyes upon him and had fallen ever deeper as they had navigated the path to adulthood together. Edmund, naturally, was totally besotted by the beautiful Alicia. He had made no secret of his plan to marry her the moment he was financially able.

Even so, certain things in life had to be done correctly, and Alicia Bartlett had insisted her beau follow the proper protocol, which began with a man-to-man talk with her father about his intentions and prospects. Dudley Bartlett was not about to give away his only daughter and a considerable dowry to just any old Tom, Dick, or Harry.

Chapter Two

During the years of their courtship, Sweetheart's Lake, which resided in the middle of Stepney Green Park, had become Alicia and Edmund's favourite place. Alicia delighted in the tranquil scene and the soft caress of cool air upon her face. The clear blue sky and serene waters always left her feeling peaceful and calm. They would take the short trip from Bethnal Green whenever they were able and picnic on the verdant, gently sloped banks of the small, usually murky brown lake.

Naturally, the two lovebirds would be accompanied by a chaperone—they were not commoners, after all. This role was often played by one of Edmund's older sisters. Oliver, on the rare occasion of him being around or sober enough, was another option, and every now and then, Dorothea Bartlett herself. But, given the circumstance of that particular early spring Sunday afternoon, Alicia and Edmund had only the ducks and other wooing couples for company.

"It will truly be a pity if they were to build terraces here," Edmund said with a long sigh as he and Alicia enjoyed their brief walk around the lake's periphery. Taking full advantage of the absence of a chaperone, Alicia had been so forward as to slip her arm through the crook of her beau's elbow. She was feeling quite grown-up and more than a little rebellious. "This place is far too beautiful to ruin with those awful worker's houses."

Ever the pragmatic one, Alicia replied, "But the slums are already filled to bursting, my love. I have heard such horrendous stories of three families and more crammed into no more than two rooms—pestilence runs rife in such conditions, and that can all too quickly spread throughout London. I'd have thought we would have learned our lesson after the Black Death."

"Of course, that is all very true, my love," Edmund said. "But this little lake holds such a dear place in our hearts. Why, it was here where we very first met."

"And it was on these very banks where we declared our undying love for one another," Alicia added. At once, she found herself caught up in her beau's sentimentality—they could build terraces somewhere else, Sweetheart's Lake was *theirs*.

"Precisely, my darling—my wish would be for this place to remain just as it is now for all eternity." Edmund ushered Alicia away from the edge of the lake and towards the woollen blanket they had spread out a little way up the smooth bank. The blanket was all the way from some little hamlet in Scotland with an unpronounceable name he had visited one summer holiday with his family. It was the perfect protection from the park's prickling grass and inquisitive ants. There, they sat themselves down and Alicia busied herself by emptying out the contents of the wicker picnic basket she had prepared the evening before.

"You are aware I spoke with Dudley . . . err, Mr. Bartlett, on Friday evening, and the nature of our conversation?" Edmund asked her.

"Of course." Alicia smiled. Edmund had informed her of his intention to speak with her father a week or so before and had been beside himself with excitement at the prospect. "What you have not told me yet is my dear father's reply to your idea of taking away his only daughter." Alicia pulled her gaze away from Edmund's almost impossibly handsome face and those eyes that fairly danced with anticipation. She lifted the cold roast beef out from the picnic basket and set it down upon one of the plain white China plates she had purloined from Mother's kitchen. Adjacent to the beef—three pounds, if it were an ounce—Alicia laid out the lettuce, veal and ham pie, a quartet of fancy apple turnovers, and the plain plum cakes she'd purchased the day before at her favourite little bakery on Old Ford Road. She also pulled out the bottle of champagne that Mother had insisted she take along—a rare but essential treat especially for the occasion.

Edmund swallowed hard. "Well, my darling," he began, his voice sounding as if someone were strangling him from the inside. "After much debate, I'm delighted to say your dear father seemed to think the whole thing was a veritably splendid idea."

"That is *delightful* news!" Throwing caution to the wind, Alicia clasped Edmund's hand in hers. She'd had no doubt her father would be only too pleased to see her betrothed to Edmund Pembroke, as he had always spoken so highly of the young man. There was also the fact Alicia could very easily have made her father's life one of living torment should he dare to say anything otherwise, and Dudley knew his spirited daughter was capable of doing so. "Thank you so much for asking him, Edmund. I know how Father can appear fearsome at times."

Edmund gave Alicia one of his special smiles—it was one that had her heart fluttering with delight and her soul melting. Wriggling his hand away from hers, Edmund dipped into the pocket of his Sunday best tailcoat and pulled out a small, black box covered in velvet. "My dear Alicia," he said as he prised open the lid of the box. "I feel completely and utterly unworthy of such a wonderful maiden as you. Not only am I besotted by your unsurpassed beauty, but I find in you a spiritual companionship worth more to me than all the world. I am not good at expressing myself, my dear Alicia, and I fear that my words are inadequate in describing the depths of my love and adoration for you. Therefore, all I will say is that it would be the greatest honour of my life if you would consider becoming my wife and making me the happiest man who has ever lived."

Although Alicia had known the moment was coming—indeed, she had played it out in her mind a thousand times and more in her daydreams—the reality of it was still far more wonderful than anything she should have possibly imagined. She felt big, fat tears forming in her deep blue eyes as her stomach flipped summersaults—it was really, *finally*, happening. Clasping trembling hands to her flushed face, Alicia stared down at the magnificent engagement ring nestled in the satin-lined box held in Edmund's shaky hand. And, while the ring itself comprised a splendid cluster of sparkling diamonds mounted atop the brightest gold she thought she had ever seen, it was what the jewellery signified that truly took Alicia's breath away.

She and her darling Edmund were to be together for always. She could scarcely believe that the day that she had longed for, for so long, was finally here.

"It is twenty-two karat gold, not Pinchbeck," Edmund ventured. He'd clearly taken Alicia's delighted lack of response for a hint of reticence. "And there is a full carat of diamond on there, too—it cost me almost a year's wage, my darling, but I can afford it now that I am to become a fully-fledged barrister . . ."

"Oh, Edmund." Alicia was overcome with emotion and could do nothing to stop the tears from rolling down her pretty cheeks. "That is such wonderful news, too."

"I believe my promotion was what swung your father's opinion in my favour," Edmund told her with a nervous smile. "So . . . don't keep me in suspense, my love. What is your answer to be?"

Alicia's reply was, of course, a resounding *yes, yes, a thousand times yes!* She felt blessed indeed to have such a wonderful man as Edmund as her fiancé.

Edmund plucked the ring from its box and slid it onto his true love's finger. Then, they sat by the side of Sweetheart's Lake and talked about their wonderful future together until the sun began to dip low towards the horizon and paint London's smoky sky a hazy, dirty shade of orange. "I will be here for you always, Alicia," Edmund promised. "I hope you know that."

A big, lavish wedding was planned for that very summer. Neither Alicia nor Edmund, or their delighted families, could see any reason at all for waiting to unite two young people who were so obviously destined to be together in the eyes of the Good Lord.

Dorothea took a great deal of the arrangements under her expert wing—the woman's organisational skills were second only to her tenacity and were particularly renowned in Bethnal Green and beyond. She forged an alliance with Edmund's mother, the equally formidable Harriett Pembroke, and between the two of them, they planned out every minute detail of their children's wedding day.

As tradition dictated, the Pembrokes were expected to pay for the whole affair, although Dudley and Dorothea agreed to foot the bill for the extravagant honeymoon in Dawlish, a picturesque seaside village in Devon. It was not that Edmund's merchant banker father couldn't afford the honeymoon, but Dudley's masculine pride insisted he do something towards giving his only daughter a jolly good send-off. Having said that, Dudley Bartlett contributed absolutely nothing else toward the wedding, other than to smoke cigars and consume large amounts of Irish whiskey with his newfound friend, Arthur Pembroke III, while the ladies went about their business.

It was just one more week before the big day, and both families had gathered at St. Dunstan's on Fleet Street for the Reading of the Banns. The church was quaint and slightly crumbling with crooked stone walls and a spectacular spire that pointed high into the sky. If felt quite solemn, with gravestones dotted sporadically throughout the churchyard, and surrounded by high oak trees. It also happened that St. Dunstan's was the church at which Alicia's parents were married, and Dudley had greased a palm or two to book the place for his daughter's nuptials. The man may have been stoic and unsentimental on the outside, but he could be prone to the occasional bout of corniness where Alicia was concerned.

"I do wish Reverend William would get on with it—we have our picnic to get to," Alicia whispered to Edmund as they sat waiting for the ancient clergyman to appear. Pastor William Jacobs had been in the diocese for as long as anyone could remember and had officiated at Dudley and Dorothea's marriage. He was also notorious for his terrible timekeeping, which was becoming progressively worse with his advancing years. This was the third time Alicia had attended the old man's church, and he'd been consistently late on each occasion. Often, the antiquated pastor's congregation would be left thinking for a good half hour or so that he may well have finally gone off to meet his maker in person!

"*Shhh*!" Dorothea hissed loudly, which served only to cause Alicia and Edmund to stifle a sudden fit of the giggles. "And why is your brother not with you?"

Alicia shrugged and cast her dramatic green eyes off to the left. There, two pews behind, Oliver sat amid Edmund's older sisters,

Diana, Frances, and Ann. He appeared to be regaling them with one of his many oft-exaggerated anecdotes of nights spent proving his worth in the ring. That he had a swollen, purple eye and split lip served only to make the dashing young man more attractive to the impressionable young ladies. They were all three easy on the eye, and hung on his every word.

"Oh, *really*." Dorothea rolled her eyes at her wayward son, who didn't notice a jot. "Can't *you* go and say something to him?" she chastised Dudley who sat quiet, and patient beside her. "That kind of lecherous behaviour is quite unbecoming for God's abode—he treats the place like it's one of his wretched gin houses."

"How on earth do you expect our son to find himself a suitable wife if you keep insisting on reining the poor chap in?" Dudley protested. "Perhaps you would prefer him to make his selection from said gin houses instead of church, my darling?" Dorothea began to say something, but clearly thought better of it.

Just like the hard, uncomfortable pews, her mother's foul mood did nothing to dampen Alicia's spirits. If her brother was to find someone who made him as happy as Edmund did her, then she would be delighted for him. In the meantime, the day was all about her impending marriage to the absolute love of her life and nothing could spoil it—not even her judgemental mother.

"I'm so sorry I'm late," the pastor mumbled as he shuffled his way up to the pulpit. He attempted to make excuses, but his voice was drowned out by the noise of two hundred or so people getting to their feet.

Alicia eyed the withered old man with great concern. There were unfounded rumours he'd actually been alive to personally witness the Great Fire itself and, although she very much doubted he'd been around in 1666, there was no question at all the man was older than dirt. Inwardly, Alicia admonished herself for the wicked thought that should the antiquated pastor die sometime in the next week before her wedding, she sincerely hoped the parish had a good standby to avoid any disruption of her big day.

Reverend Jacobs mumbled and croaked his way through the psalms and readings, most of which were lost on the congregation as they strained to hear much of what he was saying. Obscure hymns were sung and the sermon given—its theme was avoiding the temptations of pleasures of the flesh, ungodly behaviour, and, most oddly, the evils of witchcraft. Alicia listened with intent as the pastor spoke. She wondered if the subject of witches, warlocks, and black magic was particularly close to the elderly man's heart, or if he'd just forgotten it was the self-same sermon that he'd given the week before.

And so, the service dragged on until, finally, the end of that cold, uncomfortable service was in sight. Alicia shuffled her derriere about on her seat—it was beginning to feel quite numb, and she longed for the soft, luscious grass by the side of Sweetheart's Lake. She and Edmund paid close attention to the pastor as he read out the Banns. This was the third and final time for them, which meant their intention to be man and wife would be entirely official and it would be full steam ahead to their big day.

Of course, since the names were read out in alphabetical order according to the groom's surname, Alicia and Edmund had to wait a while to hear their names echo about the flaking walls of St. Dunstan's. As she waited with growing impatience, Alicia wondered how she was going to take to life as a Pembroke instead of a Bartlett, the name she'd had for nineteen years. All in all, for as daunting as the prospect seemed, Alicia decided she was going to enjoy it.

"Master Edmund Hugh Pembroke and Miss Alicia Bartlett . . ." The pastor finally got to their names and Alicia's face beamed with the broadest smile possible. Turning to Edmund, she forgot herself and clasped his hand between hers as her chest swelled with pride at the thought of finally becoming his bride.

As Edmund turned to face Alicia, she immediately saw there was something about him that didn't look quite right. His dear, sweet face appeared drained of its natural colour and, instead, had a bluish, waxen pallor to it. Edmund's eyes, which always sparkled for her, were sunken, dull, and woefully grey.

"Are you all right, my darling?" In her concern, Alicia forgot where she was, and her voice resounded throughout the church. The pastor fell silent as all heads turned in Alicia's direction—just in time to witness poor Edmund emptying his stomach of its contents all over his betrothed's best Sunday dress.

Chapter Three

The leeches hadn't worked, nor had the multitude of foul-smelling poultices Doctor Semphill had prescribed for Harriett Pembroke to administer to her son. The doctor, considered to be one of the very best in the East End of London, seemed at a complete loss as to what could possibly be wrong with the young man.

"I have observed similar symptoms in men who have travelled to India," the doctor declared rather grandly to Edmund's worried parents and Alicia. "Although, what possible miasma could travel such vast distances is simply beyond the knowledge of medical science—currently speaking, of course." The doctor scratched his head through thinning, white hair before donning his top hat and heading out to his carriage.

"There must be more that can be done for him, Doctor," Arthur Pembroke urged. His normally commanding, resonant voice quivered as he spoke.

Solemnly, the doctor shook his head. "I'm afraid all we can do now is wait—he is in God's hands now," he said. "Plenty of rest—"

"He's too damn weak to do anything else!" Harriett spat, not in the least bit embarrassed at using such an awfully crude expletive, she could always pray to the Lord for atonement later. "All he does is sleep and . . . expel whatever we try to give him to eat."

"I'm so very sorry, Mrs. Pembroke." The doctor did appear genuine. "There really is nothing else I can do at this point in time."

"Except hand us your invoice, of course," Arthur chimed in. The disgust in his tone was so palpable it made Alicia cringe.

"I shall bid you all a good day." Unwilling to get caught up in the family's grief, Doctor Semphill tipped his hat and strode out through the Pembroke's front door into the glorious summer sunshine that warmed the neatly tended lawns surrounding the house.

"Edmund wants to visit Sweetheart's Lake," Alicia told the Pembrokes as they watched the doctor's one-horse buggy disappear along the street.

"Such things can wait until he is stronger," Harriett replied with a huff. "My poor boy is in no fit state to be going anywhere—let alone to some lake with a young lady."

Alicia smarted at the barbed comment. Had Edmund not taken so suddenly and dreadfully ill, she would have become his wife in just two days' time, and part of Harriett's family. All thoughts of the wedding day which Alicia had been so eagerly anticipating had evaporated over the past week as her fiancé's condition deteriorated to the point that he was barely able to acknowledge her presence at his bedside. That Harriett and Arthur had been so kind as to allow Alicia to visit every day and spend time alone in Edmund's bedchamber was something she knew she ought to be grateful for, so Alicia decided against taking Harriet's icy comment to heart.

That night, upon returning home after a long day with Edmund, Alicia spoke secretly with her brother.

"You want me to help you do *what*?" Oliver was surprised at his sister's request, to say the least.

"I want you to help me take Edmund to our lake," Alicia repeated herself. Sometimes Oliver could be terribly infuriating.

"Against the wishes of Mr. and Mrs. Pembroke . . . *and* the doctor's orders?"

"I fear my darling Edmund is not destined to recover from whatever it is that ails him." Alicia was close to tears, but she fought them back to remain strong. "This may be his last chance to feel the sunlight on his sweet face, Oliver, and to spend time in the one place that means so much to the both of us."

"How can I possibly say no to you, my dear Alicia?" Oliver melted at the sight of his sister's heart-breaking distress. "Even if what you are proposing flies in the face of both medical opinion and good sense." A warm smile. "I shall procure a chaise from my good friend Henry Barnabus forthwith. The young rascal owes me a favour or two after our unfortunate run-in with the magistrates last month."

"You were in trouble with the magistrates?" Alicia's brow furrowed. There really was little wonder Mother and Father worried so about their firstborn child.

Oliver shook his head and grinned at her. "Nothing that concerns you right now, my sweet sister. All your thoughts must remain with your husband-to-be. And, who knows, perhaps a little fresh air by Sweetheart's Lake may have a curative influence on the poor chap?"

"Alas, if only that were true." Alicia sighed heavily. "The very least I can do for my Edmund now is to grant his final wish."

In a rare show of affection, Oliver grasped his sister's hand and squeezed it tight. "That is no way to be talking, Alicia," he reprimanded, "while ever there is breath in that young man's body and love in both your hearts, there will always be hope."

Upon hearing such kind, yet woefully misplaced words, Alicia collapsed into her brother's strong arms and wept as her heart broke into a thousand pieces. She had a hard, painful lump in her throat. How she wished his words were more than just that, and she could dare to hope for a miracle. It wasn't right that someone as good as Edmund be taken out of this world—her world would be bleak and empty without him. Alicia had dreamt of Edmund and having a lifetime of happiness together. She never conceived that she would lose her beloved before they could even be married.

But she had looked into Edmund's dulled eyes and seen Death lurking there, and she knew her true love had already acknowledged the Reaper's presence. In an instant Alicia's future had turned from magnificent to one that was bleak and full of sorrow.

"It is truly beautiful," Edmund said. His weakened voice was barely a whisper above the rustle of leaves and raucous quacking of the ducks bobbing atop the calm, glassy waters of Sweetheart's Lake. "Thank you so much for bringing me here, my dear, sweet Alicia."

Despite the warmth of the sun, Alicia's heart was numb and cold. It hurt her to see Edmund this way. He who had always been so strong now looked thin and pale. But as she looked into his soulful eyes, she saw the strength that she had always known.

Alicia cradled her beau's head in her lap. She did not care what any passers-by may think or how inappropriate such closeness would be deemed by anyone who chose to judge. Oliver sat nearby, his presence suggesting that of a mere chaperone rather than partner-in-crime.

The two of them had managed to smuggle Edmund out of the Pembroke's townhouse with relative ease. Alicia had been shocked to discover just how much weight her love had lost in less than a week of sickness. So much so, in fact, she reckoned she could have very easily carried him out through the back door hoisted over her own shoulder like a bag of cotton. As it was, she and Oliver had slung the barely conscious Edmund between them—taking an arm each—and spirited him out of the house while Harriett and Arthur had been taking high tea with Dudley and Dorothea.

Yes, Alicia and Oliver had even managed to rope their poor, unsuspecting parents in on their well-meaning subterfuge. Of course, they had not let them in on all of the nefarious details and had merely told them the Pembrokes would love to spend a pleasant Friday evening with their son's future parents-in-law.

And thus, the plot had been hatched.

Henry Barnabus had been waiting for them at the back of the house in the bright yellow chaise—the carriage was one of a dozen or so the fellow's uncle hired out for pleasure trips, and Henry would often take side jobs as postillion to pay off the numerous gambling debts he ran up at the Castle Tavern and other less than wholesome dens of iniquity about London.

The chaise itself was pulled by a pair of stocky, young, piebald mares, one of whom had decided to relieve itself the moment they had arrived in the carriage waiting area of Stepney Green Park. Henry didn't seem at all concerned by the mess or the smell and sat patiently while Edmund enjoyed the sunset over the small lake.

"It is *our* place, my darling Edmund," Alicia said softly as she brushed away a stray strand of hair from his fevered brow. That Edmund was alert enough to be appreciative of his surroundings and speak to her was a miracle all in itself, although it offered poor Alicia the cruel vein of hope he may just live to become her husband after all.

"As it will always be," Edmund replied. His voice sounded dreamy, as if he were already far, far away. "Whenever I think of you, I think of this magical place, and all of the wonderful times we have enjoyed here with each other."

Alicia was unsure as to how she managed to fight back the tears. "And we will enjoy so many more, my love," she said.

Somehow, through his weakness, Edmund struggled to sit upright, although he leaned what little weight remained in him against Alicia. Sadly, he shook his head. "I'm afraid I know when I am beaten, my dear, sweet Alicia," he told her with a long, rattling sigh. "None of us can choose when our time on earth ends, and it's time for me to return to my maker. Whatever malaise has taken over my humours has me done for, I fear. I am so terribly weak and unbelievably weary—I find the very process of living so incredibly exhausting. All I wish to do now is fall asleep dreaming of you and never awaken."

"Please don't talk like that," Alicia begged of him. "You are strong, Edmund, and you *will* recover from this beastly illness."

"One look into your beautiful eyes tells me that you know in your dear heart that is not true." Edmund was quite firm on the matter. "But I know you feel you must lie to me for my sake and, if I may be so bold as to venture, yours also. My time is almost done on this earth, Alicia, and it will behove you to admit it, at least to yourself, so we may say our final goodbyes." So saying, Edmund rested a hand upon Alicia's. His weak, fevered fingers absently fiddled with the engagement ring he'd put there what seemed like a lifetime ago.

"I can't . . ." Alicia whimpered as the lump in her throat grew bigger.

"But you *must*," Edmund insisted. "Our time here on Earth is short enough as it is, and for some reason, God has decreed mine to be shorter than any of us had expected—I like to think He has other plans for me, none of which I am to be party to just yet. I don't know why, and I pled with the Lord to allow me the privilege to watch over you and keep you safe. The Lord spoke peace to my soul, and I felt of His great love for you. I know that God is even more concerned about your welfare than I am, and so I put my trust in His goodness." Pausing to catch his breath, Edmund's chest wheezed and rattled like that of some decrepit old crone succumbing to the plague. "I will always be here for you, my love." Edmund pointed with his chin toward Sweetheart's Lake. The rays of the setting sun twinkled and danced upon its waters like myriad faeries making merry. "Whenever you feel the need to be with me, come to our place and think of me. I promise I'll never be too far away."

"Oh, Edmund," Alicia sobbed. "Don't talk that way. I'm not ready to say goodbye."

"Please don't cry, my darling Alicia." As Edmund gazed into her piercing blue eyes, Alicia saw the old, familiar shine within his as they sparkled brightly for her one last time. "And don't forget, I'll always love you."

Alicia leant down to kiss him gently on the lips. It was the first time their lips had ever met and would also be the last time they would meet during mortal life. The tears streamed from Alicia's face, and landed on Edmund's, making it appear that he too was weeping. But by this stage, his strength had almost seeped out of him.

With a protracted, fatigued sigh, Edmund slumped into Alicia's arms and his body fell limp.

Alicia gently shook his lifeless body, but there was no response. Alicia's stomach lurched as realisation hit her. Her tears streamed down her cheeks, and she pressed her forehead into her beloved's shoulder, her tears rolling down to stain Edmund's coat. Her throat was impossibly tight, and a strange coldness had taken over her body. Alicia wondered if she—if anything—would ever feel right again. Alicia held on to her beau there on the banks of Sweetheart's Lake until the sun vanished below London's chimney pots and dusk turned all too quickly to night. She felt a loneliness beyond anything that she had ever experienced before. How could she say goodbye to her beloved, not even knowing when, or if, they would ever meet again.

Chapter Four

London, England. 1819

"I must apologise for having not visited in a while." Fiddling with the diamond engagement ring she'd not had the heart to take from her finger, Alicia spoke quietly lest others in the park think her quite mad and she found herself whisked off to join the awful inmates who occupied Bedlam Insane Asylum. Stepney Green Park was a place for courting couples, not unwed young women who talk to small lakes.

Alicia shivered at a faint, gentle breeze. Standing in deep contemplation on the precise spot where, just four years before, she had bid a final farewell to her beloved Edmund, Alicia regarded with envy the happy young couples who strolled so carefree and gay around the lake Edmund had declared to be theirs. An emptiness had eaten away at her ever since that fatal day that her beloved was taken from her.

Alicia's reflection from the lake didn't seem as beautiful and carefree as it had once been. Alicia felt like she was a shadow of the woman that she used to be, and she wondered whether life would ever become tolerable for her again. She so dreadfully missed those simpler, more carefree days when she would spend hours on end at the lake with her beloved. *Maybe I'm just tired*, Alicia thought. She had stayed up late writing a poem only to get up again three short, restless hours later.

She often daydreamed of being a captivating writer someday, but that longed for day was still far in the future.

The Pembrokes had never found it in their hearts to forgive Alicia for sneaking their precious son from the house against doctor's orders that day. In her grief, and desperate to lay blame, Harriett had even gone so far as to suggest—quite publicly—Alicia was *solely* responsible for her son's untimely demise. The poor woman had also deluded herself into believing Edmund had been perfectly capable of recovering from his sickness, and Alicia and her wicked brother's actions had added so much stress to his weakened body he'd simply given up. The two families had not spoken from that day on, and had even managed to maintain a detached, stony silence at poor Edmund's funeral.

Of course, life had carried on around Alicia as she wrapped herself up in the inconsolable grief of the loss of her one true love. King George III was still as mad as the proverbial hatter, while his idiot son, the prince regent, was making a terrible mockery of the crown by dividing the country with his ludicrous excesses and public frippery. Steam engines continued to grow in popularity and seemed to be taking over the factories and mills up and down the country—every industrialised city was purported to be choking to death in the thick smoke the ghastly things belched out night and day; it was a terrible blight no longer confined to London. The Luddites had finally been defeated once and for all, and their ringleaders shipped off to the new colony known as Australia, which was a strange, inhospitable land filled with the most unbelievable creatures many believed to be God's most embarrassing mistakes. There really was no halting the progress of England's burgeoning industries and ruthless expansion of the Empire.

The disease from India that had killed Alicia's dear Edmund was eventually given a name—cholera—and was rife around London. So much so, the Bartletts were seriously considering a move to the country to avoid it. The sickness had been declared an actual pandemic and was compared most unfavourably to the Great Plague that had decimated a great deal of Europe only a couple of centuries before. Cholera appeared to be an especially classless ailment and was not solely confined to the slum housing and workhouses. Indeed, Alicia had lost a few of the friends she had made during her years at finishing school, and her father had mourned more than a handful of close business acquaintances. And still, the doctors and the very best the scientific community had to offer could only hazard vague guesses at what was causing the awful sickness that laid waste to even the strongest of men within a matter of days.

"You have nothing to apologise for, my darling," Edmund reassured her from his place beneath the water. "It has been four years since my passing—I'd say it was high time for you to be moving on with your life."

Alicia stared deep into the shimmering water of Sweetheart's Lake. There, she saw Edmund's familiar, sweet face, sparkling eyes, and spectacular moustache, and he looked as well and healthful as before he had been taken so terribly ill in the church. From the day of his death, Alicia had made her pilgrimage every Sunday—weather willing—to their place by the lake to speak with her dear fiancé. Having him there for her ensured she never felt lonely, sad, or in need of a dear friend.

And, it had come as little surprise to have Edmund speaking back to her.

At first, Alicia had thought herself to be either a lunatic or imagined that her grief was playing cruel tricks upon her. But, as time went by, Alicia realised Edmund was keeping his promise to always be there for her and that brought her a great deal of comfort in her times of need.

Mother had given Alicia a year to mourn before suggesting she find a more wholesome way to spend the remainder of the Lord's Day after church.

"What would you rather I do, Mother?" Alicia was fond of countering. "Take up pugilism and gin drinking with my rapscallion brother?"

"I more had in mind shuttlecock." Dorothea's go-to retort had never ceased to amuse Alicia. She could no more see herself prancing about a grassy court with other *eligible ladies of virtue* than she could give up the visits to her darling Edmund. Besides, how could she possibly explain to her worried parents she was not really alone, as she was enjoying such wonderful conversations with her lost love?

But, as time wore on, and Alicia became aware of life racing by without her, her visits to the lake had become less frequent.

And this was to be her last.

"I have met a gentleman who has captured my heart. His name is Hilary," Alicia blurted out. It felt good to relieve herself of the burden of the secret she'd forced herself to keep from Edmund for almost a year. "Doctor Hilary St. John. He knows all about you and understands fully why I cannot bear to part with the ring you placed upon my finger. He tells me he is prepared to wait a lifetime for my love if that is what it takes. Nonetheless, we are to be married in August."

Edmund smiled and appeared to be quite pleased for her. "A doctor, you say?" he said. "That is the most wonderful news, my love. All I want for you is a long life of happiness and joy and for you to be showered with love. May I enquire as to where you met such a worthy young fellow?"

Alicia began to feel more than a little bit awkward discussing such matters with the ghost of the man she was supposed to have married—she had made the logical assumption Edmund was a ghost early on in their new relationship and hadn't thought it appropriate to ask. "It was at a society dance in Whitehall—Mother insisted I attend rather than spend the remainder of my life sulking within the confines of my bedchamber."

"Of course she did." Edmund laughed. "How I miss dear Dorothea—she will make a most fearsome mother-in-law when you marry this Hilary chap."

"She was supposed to be *your* mother-in-law, Edmund." Raw emotion swept through Alicia, and immediately she felt guilty at planning her life with someone other than him. "I shall not be visiting you again, Edmund," she told him, her voice flat, emotionless.

"I knew this time would come." Edmund sounded far older than his years; his words were those of some wise old sage. "I am so pleased you are ready to move on, Alicia. I just want you to be happy."

"I shall miss you terribly, Edmund, and I shall miss being able to talk with you as we have since . . ."

"Since my death?" Edmund added as if the event was of so little consequence. "It is quite acceptable for you to say the word, Alicia—it is a fact I have had four years to come to terms with. We may be on different sides of the veil, but you will always be a dear friend to me."

"I would consider myself being untrue to Hilary should we continue our dalliances," Alicia explained to Edmund with great sadness. "Especially here, and especially like this. I will have to give my husband-to-be my full attention and all of my heart—I do hope you can find it within yourself to understand."

"Of course, I understand, my darling Alicia. But do remember, Sweetheart's Lake will always belong to us, my love," Edmund said with a fond smile. "And I will always be here . . . just in case you ever need me."

Alicia's attempt to reply was choked by the tears that rose into her soulful eyes and trickled down her throat and, for the briefest of moments she thought—*hoped*—her beloved Edmund would rise up out of the water and take her in his arms for one last time.

Sadly, that was not to be.

"Goodbye, Alicia, my darling." Edmund's handsome, smiling face began to fade away beneath the water of Sweetheart's Lake.

"Farewell, Edmund, love of my life," Alicia replied. It took every single ounce of strength she possessed not to jump into the cold, murky water after him. It was only the thought of being fished out of the lake a soggy, bedraggled mess to be carted off forthwith to the insane asylum that prevented such a foolish action. Instead, Alicia composed herself and watched with a heavy heart as Edmund's face and sparkling eyes vanished from sight.

Before she turned to go, Alicia slipped the engagement ring from her finger, touched it briefly to her lips for one last, tender kiss, and then tossed it into Sweetheart's Lake. She wanted it to be with Edmund and knew in her heart he would take good care of it.

Alicia would never forget the kind, pure, and sincere man that was her Edmund. She would remember him with a unique, sweet sadness. However, it really was time for her to move on with her life and embrace whatever it had in store for her.

Chapter Five

Alicia Bartlett became Mrs. Alicia St. John, a doctor's wife, on the fourteenth day of August of that year. They married at Christ Church in Spitalfields, having missed out on St. Dunstan's on account of the place being torn down two years previously. Its rapidly crumbling foundations were considered too dangerous for any fit purpose. Reverend Jacobs had finally, reluctantly shuffled off his mortal coil a month or two before the demolition commenced. He was struck down, along with a dozen or so of his loyal parishioners, by the dreaded cholera as it tightened its deadly grip upon London. There were whispered rumours about the city that the old parson's ghost could be seen shuffling about the church's ruins as if it were desperately searching for something.

Alicia quite liked Spitalfields, as it was a similarly well-to-do town as Bethnal Green. Hilary had spent the entirety of his thirty years of life in the place, growing up as the only son of Jonathon and Sarah St. John. Hilary's father was a doctor, as was his grandfather before him, so it had been expected he follow in the family footsteps, which was a tradition he threw himself into with aplomb. In fact, the young doctor had secured himself a somewhat prestigious position working alongside the king's physicians as they attempted to find a cure for the ailing, lunatic monarch.

But that was not what had caused Alicia to gravitate toward Hilary upon making his acquaintance. Nor was it his tall, strong frame, incredibly handsome face, and impeccable dress sense. The young man was only very rarely seen without his smart suit, top hat, and important-looking fob watch his grandfather had gifted upon the occasion of his taking the Hippocratic Oath. No, it was Hilary's endless patience with Alicia and the fact he didn't seem to mind one jot whenever she spoke to him about Edmund. Although, she hadn't gone so far as to relate to her new beau that she spoke to her deceased fiancé in the lake and that his love for her was entirely unconditional. Alicia loved Hilary too, of course she did, although it was subtly different from the all-consuming emotion she had held for Edmund—such love only came along once in a lifetime.

They bought a modest two-storey cottage in Spitalfields, which was just around the corner from Hilary's parents' rather grander mansion and a touch under two miles away from the Bartlett's home in Bethnal Green—less than an hour away by carriage, or half that by horseback. It meant Dorothea and Dudley were regular visitors to their daughter's new home, and even Oliver would call by on occasion. He and Hilary seemed to get along famously. They shared a mutual love of boxing, although the good doctor had given up his active participation in the sport shortly after leaving university.

All in all, the two families got along splendidly, and married life was idyllic for Alicia. She became so delightfully immersed in her life's new chapter as a physician's wife, she barely had time to think about Edmund at all much less miss her regular visits to see him at Sweetheart's Lake. The early morning hours often found her at her desk working diligently on her writing by the flickering light of the oil lamp.

They had been married a touch over four months when Hilary first introduced Alicia to his colleague, Dr. Gregory Sedgewick, with whom he worked alongside the king's physicians. Gregory was a thin, weaselly character with a pinched face and dark, narrow eyes. He wore a full, bushy black beard that stretched all the way down to his chest and, since he had a rather unpleasant tendency to speak with his mouth full, it was often festooned with tiny fragments of food. Alicia was embarrassed she had taken an instant dislike to Gregory—although she thought she hid it well from both he and her husband—even though the young man carried an irresistible charm and intelligent wit about him. Hilary informed her the ladies actually often found that to be quite irresistible.

"It is a pleasure to meet you at last," Gregory said as he lifted Alicia's hand to his lips for the customary light kiss.

"Likewise, Dr. Sedgewick," Alicia cringed a little at the bristly scratch of the man's wiry beard upon the soft skin at the back of her hand.

"Please, call me Gregory," the young doctor insisted as he relinquished her hand and removed his top hat. "I would hate to think we need to be so formal."

"Gregory it is, then." Alicia smiled and ushered the man toward the cosy dining room. As she did so, she noticed his eyes dart to the sprig of mistletoe secured to the crossbeam over the doorway and espied the expectant glint in his eyes. Deftly, she sidestepped the doctor and made her way into the kitchen before he could lay claim to the ages-old tradition.

Alicia had always loved Christmastide, or at least she had until Edmund's passing; after that, she'd found the festivities somewhat hollow and insincere. Her first Christmastide with Hilary was to be different, though, being the start of a whole new era in her life. Indeed, Alicia was already feeling in the spirit, thanks in part to the wassailers who had woken her up at the crack of dawn with their merry singing at her doorstep and her husband's almost child-like excitement about the season.

With just three days to go before the big day, Alicia had her new home decorated with holly and laurel from the garden, rosemary and bay from Hilary's mother's herb garden and, of course, the mistletoe, which she had picked herself from the apple orchard at the end of the road to place strategically about the cottage. Later, on the eve of Christmas itself, she would add gold paper and silk to the décor and make final preparations for the family dinner she had volunteered to host for both her family and her husband's. Goose had always been a firm favourite, and Alicia relished the opportunity to roast one all by herself.

To add the finishing touch to the festive scene in Alicia's dining room, a fat Yule log crackled and spat in the open fireplace.

"You do have plenty of rosemary," Gregory said as he took his seat at the table and Alicia walked in with a huge, steaming ham. Hilary had invited his colleague over for light supper and sherry—it was kind of a tradition of theirs and, since the doctor had no family of his own and would be spending Christmas day alone, Hilary had felt obliged. "And bay—the two are herbs of fertility, don't you know?" He fixed Alicia with such a lascivious expression she wished she'd delayed coming back from the kitchen a minute or two longer.

"There is no impending pitter-patter of tiny feet, if that's what you are hinting at, my good friend," Hilary declared with a hearty laugh. "My darling Alicia has yet to complete her first novel. After that, there will be plenty of time for the rearing of St. John offspring, I think."

"You are a writer?" Gregory appeared genuinely interested in the fact. "Pray tell—what you are writing, my dear?"

Alicia felt her cheeks flush a little. She had only just begun working on her novel and was embarrassed to so much as discuss it. She had discovered Jane Austen many years ago and had been devastated by the author's death only a couple of years after Edmund's. Alicia had so fallen in love with her worlds and characters she was inspired to create her own. Whether or not she would ever be able to live up to Ms. Austen's heady literary heights remained to be seen, since Alicia had not even allowed her husband to read any of her work thus far. "It is a convoluted tale of romance and heartbreak," Alicia informed Gregory. "I have set it among the lower-class slums and workhouses of London. I feel the affluent and countryside gentry have had more than enough written about them. Wouldn't you agree, Gregory?"

The doctor nodded. "I am familiar with the works of Jane Austen, of course, but I must profess to harbouring a preference for Walter Scott and Mary Shelley. Tell me, my dear, have you read *Frankenstein* yet?"

Alicia could barely suppress the shudder that rippled through her body. It was a chill that ran straight through to her very core despite the warmth of the fire. "I have no desire to read such ghoulish tales, thank you very much," she told Gregory. "Lunatic doctors stealing cadavers and bringing dead things back to life—it all sounds rather too gruesome and ungodly for my tastes."

"Perhaps Miss Shelley's yarn is not as fictional as you may think," Hilary chipped in with a sly grin. "Who knows what we lunatic doctors get up to behind closed doors?"

"Indeed." Joining in with the teasing, Gregory was showing a little warmth at last. "With all the abundant, fresh cholera corpses at our disposal, who knows what heinous works are afoot in the name of the king?"

"Is that what keeps my husband from me?" Alicia asked with a cheeky smile playing upon her full lips. She was only just getting used to the long hours Hilary was forced to keep between his time at the palace and the teaching hospital. "Reanimating the dead who, one would imagine, have little desire to experience life again in such a terrible way?"

"Expanding the realms of medical science is a *very* important business. As the wife of a physician, I'm sure you can appreciate such a fundamental fact." Gregory was beginning to sound a little too condescending, which Alicia didn't care for at all.

"My wife may not be a physician, but she certainly has the wherewithal to understand the magnitude of our work, Gregory. Especially in such times under the spectre of an awful disease we are only able to treat with leeches and quack medicines that kill almost as many as the cholera itself." Hilary sprang to Alicia's defence with chivalrous vigour. "She is also painfully aware of the importance of finding a cure for what ails King George before that feebleminded son of his destroys the monarchy once and for all and throws the Empire open to a whole host of potential marauders."

"Alas, we are none the wiser on that particular count now than we were eight years ago." Gregory rolled his eyes. "All we know is that the poor old chap's urine is an alarmingly unnatural shade of blue and he is, of course, stark raving mad."

"We do prefer to use the word *lunatic*," Hilary explained to Alicia with a sardonic smile. "It's a far more civilised description, don't you think?"

Gregory scoffed at his colleague's playful chastisement. "It is a word derived from *lunar*, which was coined in the dark ages to suggest the full moon was the cause of madness. It is hardly what I would call civilised, my dear Hilary." He laughed at his own witticism, and Hilary and Alicia laughed along with him for the sake of politeness.

The more the three of them talked, the more of Alicia began to see through Gregory's obnoxious exterior and caught a touch more of the gentleman's innate charm that Hilary had spoken of. The man clearly possessed an immense intelligence and was incredibly wide read about literature, politics, world events, and, as one would expect, medicine. He'd also travelled a lot in his formative years—India, post-revolution America, France, Germany, and Russia to name but a few—and made it his business to keep up with all of the goings-on in each one of those countries. It also turned out, Gregory was quite the ninepin player—a game Alicia had loved to play on her father's manicured back lawn in the warm, hazy summer days of her childhood. And, before she knew what was what, Alicia had agreed to play a game or two with Gregory when his hectic schedule permitted.

When the evening finally came to an end, Alicia was genuinely sad to see Gregory leave. His company had been most stimulating, and she didn't believe she had laughed as loud or quite so much since . . .

Edmund.

Alicia forced herself to push the sadness aside and embrace the bonhomie of the occasion. She even made Gregory cross his heart and hope to die he would visit with them again over the holiday season.

"It would be an honour," Gregory replied with a wide grin beneath the now amusingly untidy bush of his beard. "Thank you for welcoming me into your home, my dear, sweet Alicia." Gregory kissed the back of her hand again, and Alicia didn't find it quite as objectionable as the first time. "You are the perfect match for my good friend here." The doctor pointed a finger at the grinning Hilary. "He definitely deserves a wife as wonderful as you, and I predict you will both make the most gorgeous children on God's green Earth!"

With that, Gregory walked down the narrow pathway to where a yellow chaise carriage awaited. "He has digs in Whitechapel," Hilary explained as they waved Gregory off from the stoop. "He'll be there before we retire to our bedchamber, my darling." Placing an arm about Alicia's shoulders, he ushered her back into the welcoming warmth of their home. "Thank you for tolerating Dr. Sedgewick—I know the man can be dreadfully boorish on occasion."

Alicia laughed and smiled up at her wonderful, handsome husband. She loved how he would drape a strong, warm arm around her and pull her close; it made her feel so delightfully safe. "He really is a nice young man beneath all that bluster, Hilary. I think you do not give him enough credit. I'm sure he will find himself a suitable match someday very soon."

"I do hope you are right, my darling," Hilary replied as Alicia steered him toward the dining room. There, the table was still cluttered with the remnants of their evening's entertaining. "Let us leave the clearing away for the morning," he said. "We have to be up early to visit the orphanage with our Christmastide gifts—did I tell you the St. Johns have been patrons of the Foundling Hospital for three generations?"

Alicia nodded. Yes, her husband had regaled her with tales of his family's generous philanthropy on numerous occasions; it was a fact of which he was exceptionally proud. "I'm sure it can wait 'til the morning, my love," she agreed. "After all the good food and exceptional company, I am more than ready to retire for the night."

While Alicia blew out the candles, Hilary locked the doors and made his way upstairs. Before too long, Alicia had fallen fast asleep in her husband's strong, safe arms. Her head resting upon his warm, broad chest and, for the first time since their wedding day, she dreamt of Sweetheart's Lake.

Chapter Six

JANUARY 1820

Christmastide came and went all too quickly, and everyone agreed Alicia's first time hosting Christmas dinner was, without a doubt, a resounding success. The goose was cooked to perfection, the trimmings were all simply divine, and the company was wonderful. Alicia's parents, Oliver, Doctor and Mrs. St. John, all enjoyed one another's company—and Oliver and Hilary even put on a display of boxing skills that had everyone at the edge of their seats, much to the horror of Dorothea.

Alicia and Hilary saw in the New Year at her parent's house in Bethnal Green. It was a formal affair with many of Dudley Bartlett's legal associates and clients in attendance, which meant Alicia's often unpredictable brother was under strict instruction to restrict his wine intake and advances on the ladies present—eligible and otherwise. Alicia was obliged to buy a fancy new dress for the occasion. With her mother's expert guidance, she had opted for a gorgeous, incredibly feminine gown in pale pink silk with an outer layer of ornately decorated white netting. Mother had declared her daughter to be the belle of the ball! Naturally, Alicia eschewed a bonnet, what with being a married woman and all, and wore her fair hair up with thin ringlets framing her pretty face. Hilary couldn't stop telling her all night long just how proud he was to have her on his arm as they danced together to Mozart, Pleyel, Naderman, and everyone's favourite, Beethoven.

But, for as much as all the festivities and socialising had Alicia feeling vibrant and more alive than she had in many a year, she was grateful when it was all over. More than anything, she looked forward to getting back to her normal, everyday life as a physician's wife and would-be author of the literary world's next great romance novel.

"I truly wish I didn't have to return to work so soon," Hilary said as they made ready for bed. He wore his nightgown beneath the luscious kimono-style dressing gown his parents had gifted him, while Alicia buried herself amongst the blankets to stave off the chill winter air that pervaded the bedchamber; her thin linen shift was less than effective in keeping her warm all by itself. "I have had a wonderful time being home with you, my love."

"It has been an absolute delight being able to spend time with you, too," Alicia agreed. "Do you realise this Christmastide has been the longest amount of time we have spent together since our honeymoon?"

"I am all too aware of that fact," Hilary said with a sigh. "The career I have chosen takes me away from my beautiful new bride for so many hours in every day."

Alicia smiled at her husband as he slipped off his dressing gown and clambered between the cold bedsheets beside her. "At least it gives me something to look forward to throughout my day," she said with firmness in her voice.

"If only I were fit for any kind of conversation when I do finally return home." Hilary's attempt at humour fell a little flat. "You have shown great patience with me for virtually falling asleep in my supper every night."

"You are working for the King of England," Alicia reassured him. "I'm sure I can make allowances for such essential research given all that is at stake."

"I wouldn't quite describe it as *research*, my darling." Hilary laughed softly, as if at some obscure, personal joke only he could possibly find to be amusing. "What we are doing is more about guesswork and stabbing around in the dark while praying we stumble across the answer. Gregory and I were startled to discover, prior to the holiday, the king's physicians had only just ruled out witchcraft as a probable cause!"

"Are we still living in the Middle Ages?" Alicia giggled. "That is simply outrageous!"

"We are working on a diagnosis that the king's ailment is a brain fever, although that doesn't explain his sapphire-blue wastewater at all. Or perhaps it is merely a chronic imbalance in his humours—but bleeding him didn't seem to have any effect other than to make him even more cantankerous and delusional than before. The poor old man spent much of November and December believing he still owned America and the Tea Party never happened!"

"You and Gregory are fine, upstanding doctors," Alicia said with a wide, sleepy yawn. "I have every confidence you will both find a cure for our dear king before too long—and well before it is too late to seat his royal derriere back on the throne where it belongs." She chuckled at her risqué joke at the monarch's expense, which had Hilary smiling.

"I really ought to go to sleep now, my love." Hilary leaned across to the nightstand and blew out the fat, white candle that flickered there. "I have arranged for the knocker-upper to do his duty well before cockcrow—I must be at the palace before dawn. I promise to try not to disturb you as I leave."

"But you *must*," Alicia insisted. She could no longer see her husband, as their room was so very pitch-black without the benefit of the candle's yellow flame. "If I am not to see you 'til the late hours, then grant me at least a little time in the morning. I can always return to our bed to catch up on my sleep before starting my day proper."

"Very well." Hilary sounded bone weary. It was as if the very act of climbing into bed had exhausted him. "I shall look forward to seeing you in the morning, my darling."

"Sleep well, my sweet husband," Alicia said as she, too, succumbed to the soft embrace of a dreamless slumber.

Chapter Seven

A strident, insistent thumping at the cottage door roused both Alicia and Hilary from their sleep.

"What the—?" Hilary groaned as he struggled to wake up.

"Is it morning already?" Alicia asked as she rubbed at her eyes. It was still inky black in their bedchamber but given the time of year and her husband's scheduled early start, that came as little surprise.

"I don't think so," Hilary said as he groped about on the nightstand for the matchbox. "Whoever it is, it must be some kind of emergency."

The banging on the door continued. Each resolute thump echoed throughout the night-clad cottage, as if its very foundations were rattling. Alicia sat up in bed, reluctant to swing her feet out from beneath the warmth of the blankets.

"You stay here, my love," Hilary instructed as, finally, he located the matches and lit the bedside candle. "It's likely some medical emergency or other—there's no need for us both to get up."

A wave of fear forced its way down Alicia's spine as, in an instant, the entire house filled with the sound of a deafening crash and splintering of wood. Whoever had been pounding upon the door had clearly lost their patience at being left waiting.

There came the noise of heavy, purposeful footsteps on the wooden stairs.

Panicking, Hilary darted across the bedchamber to the oak wardrobe that stood sentry in the corner and flung open the door. As he scrabbled around inside its barely lit, gloomy interior for his sword or pistol, the bedchamber door flew open. In stormed a quartet of Royal Horse Guards with their swords drawn and metal breastplates glinting in the flickering yellow light of the solitary candle by the bed. They had on their tall, steel helmets, crested by upright, bristly black fur, and looked rather dapper in their pristine white pantaloons and shiny black riding boots.

Bravely, Hilary spun around and faced those who had rudely interrupted his much-needed sleep. He brandished his rapier sword with lethal intent, and, although he was clad only in his nightshirt, he managed to appear quite menacing as he faced the guards.

The guards didn't hesitate in the slightest at Hilary's defiant stance, and they moved in on him as Alicia gasped in horror from the bed. The guard nearest to Hilary engaged him with his own long, sharp sword, and the harsh noise of the clash of metal upon metal reverberated around the bedchamber. Determined to defend his home and beloved wife—and not caring a jot that the intruders may well have been on the king's business—Hilary countered with an upwards parry. This caught his skilled opponent off guard and forced him to take a step backwards. Encouraged by the tiny victory, Hilary thrust forward towards the fellow's midriff with the keen tip of his rapier aimed at the unprotected belly just below the bottom hem of the guard's breastplate.

Another of the guards stepped up and, with one mighty swipe, deflected Hilary's sword away from his colleague.

Hilary staggered to the left under the sheer force of the guard's interference. He fought hard to keep hold of his own sword. The brutal blow had sent vibrations up the length of the metal and jarred every joint in his hand and arm—all the way to his shoulder, which throbbed its complaint. Nonetheless, Hilary recovered quickly and brought his sword around to see the guards advancing upon him with their swords aimed directly at his heart.

"*Stop this*!" The guard nearest the door shouted above the clank of steel and animalistic grunts. It was difficult to ascertain whether he was the leader of the four, or if he had merely taken it upon himself to assume the role. The quartet were all identically dressed and had no medals, ribbons, or insignia to give away rank or superiority that Alicia could make out in the dim light of her bedchamber. Regardless, the two guards rounding on her poor husband took a step back. Their vicious swords remained drawn and pointed at Hilary as if accusing him of some unspeakably heinous deed. The guard who had thus far done very little other than storm into the room, froze on the spot with his weapon gripped tightly in his hand and pointed at the wooden floor. Alicia thought he appeared to be the youngest of the four and wondered if the Royal Horse Guards took on apprentices.

"Doctor Hilary St. John." As the lead guard took several steps toward Hilary, the hard soles of his shiny boots thumped upon the floor like small, ominous claps of thunder. "You are to come with us."

"What the dickens is the meaning of this?" Hilary said as he lowered his sword. His eyed the swords that were aimed at his heart with both puzzlement and fear. Even as a skilled swordsman, he clearly had the good sense to know when he was outnumbered and beaten.

Alicia allowed herself to breathe out a small sigh of relief. Her brave husband's gallantry was a delight to behold, but she dreaded the thought of watching four Royal Horse Guards run him through with their swords while she sat there helplessly in her bed. "There must be some mistake," she ventured, and was surprised at just how strong and forceful her voice sounded. She was terrified, of course, but didn't want the guards to know that.

"There has been no mistake, madam," the youngest guard told her. He had kind eyes, an apologetic smile, and Alicia very much doubted he had even begun to shave, such was his youth. Also, he did seem quite bashful at finding himself in a lady's bedchamber at such a late hour.

"We are placing you under arrest," the lead guard said to Hilary. His tone was direct and matter of fact. "By orders of the Prince Regent, George IV, you are to accompany us to the Tower of London, where you are to face trial for high treason."

Alicia gasped at the man's wicked words. Her dear, darling Hilary accused of treason?! "My husband is a good man." She fought back the tears to maintain the forcefulness in her voice. "He is a kind and charitable doctor—he has tended to the king for many years. There really has been a most terrible blunder here."

"I can assure you there has been no mistake, Mrs. St. John." The lead guard turned his attention to Alicia, his eyes respectfully downturned to avoid gazing directly at a lady not only in her night-time attire but also in her bed. "Our orders are quite precise, and they come directly from the palace itself. You would be best advised not to interfere with the crown's affairs and allow us to get on with our job."

"I will go with them without putting up a fight, Alicia," Hilary said quietly as he dropped his sword to the bedchamber floor. His nervousness showed through his trembling voice. The resonant *clank* it made as it rattled against the thick, oak boards was the abject sound of defeat. "I promise you I am no more guilty of treason than any other law-abiding fellow you could care to mention. I'm quite sure I will get to the bottom of whatever mix-up has occurred here and have it all sorted out in two shakes of a lamb's tail. The prince regent himself knows I am a good man and has often praised the work of myself and Dr. Sedgewick in respect to our search for the elusive cure for his father."

"Take him away," the lead guard grunted, and the two who had engaged Hilary sheathed their swords and took him by an arm each. "There ought to be no reason for us to shackle or manacle him." He looked with spite directly into Hilary's eyes as he delivered what was obviously intended to be a threat. "Isn't that so, Dr. St. John?"

"I will accompany you in peace, sir," Hilary replied.

"Hilary . . ." Alicia began, but the words simply failed her. Just what was one supposed to say on the occasion of one's husband's arrest by the crown? It was certainly a subject Miss Chapman-Boothe had neglected to cover in finishing school, although her deportment classes had been quite outstanding.

"Don't worry yourself, my love," Hilary reassured his wife as the guards escorted him from the bedchamber, but lines of worry furrowed his brow. "All will be well—that much I can promise you."

"I shall ride to inform my father post-haste," Alicia told him and, forgetting she had uninvited guests of the male persuasion still in her room, swung her legs out from beneath the bedsheets. "He will know what has to be done!"

"I would advise that keeps 'til the morning, madam." The lead guard's tone left Alicia under the impression that he was giving her an order and not making a friendly suggestion.

Alicia gave the guard a compliant smile and took a little selfish pleasure at the pompous man's embarrassment as his eyes accidentally caught a glimpse of her delicate bare toes and uncovered ankle as she slipped them back beneath the bedsheets. "Very well," she said softly, "but rest assured, I shall be at the tower by cockcrow with my father, who is a prominent and well-respected barrister."

"Do be sure to let Gregory know what has happened to me, too," Hilary said over his shoulder as the guards frog marched him towards the stairs with his bare soles hardly touching the floor at all. "Perhaps he will speak to Prince George and have this whole misunderstanding ironed out even before cockcrow."

Alicia promised her husband she would waste no time in making her way to Whitechapel to rally Dr. Sedgewick. They were certain that he would do whatever was within his power to secure Hilary's release. Despite her initial reserve towards her husband's colleague, Alicia had begun to see the pleasant personality beneath his prickly, gaunt exterior. She also knew in her heart he would do anything and everything to come to her husband's aid; they were not only great colleagues, but good friends, too.

Biting back her tears, Alicia slipped from her bed, which was still warm from her beloved husband's body, and followed the sorry procession down the stairs. From a safe distance, she watched forlornly as the two strapping Royal Horse Guards manhandled Hilary into the prison carriage. It was a horrid, black affair complete with iron bars and a pair of huge, sinister-looking horses, who were as black as the night that surrounded them.

Distraught, Alicia watched them go until they were swallowed up by the darkness of the small hours. She stood there all alone on the doorstep of her lovely little cottage for a long time after the rhythmic *clip-clop-clip* of the horses' hooves ceased echoing through the air.

Chapter Eight

Of course, Alicia had been unable to sleep a wink. Having been forced to watch as her dear husband was carted off in such an unceremonious fashion by the Royal Horse Guards, her poor mind was fairly reeling from the brutality of the invasion into her home. She did, however, take the lead guard's advice and wait until the morning before venturing out to begin her long day to help Hilary in his dire hour of need.

It broke Alicia's heart too much to return to her bed, so she knelt by it and poured out her heart to the Lord with tears streaming down her cheeks. Afterwards she climbed into bed where she lay sniffling miserably as she continued to cry unto the Lord. Slowly, a gentle peace began to fill her soul. For the first time in quite a while, she found herself wishing she had Edmund to confide in. Then, as the sun peeped up over the horizon, Alicia made the short walk to Hilary's parent's house. Here she planned to procure a horse and ride to Bethnal Green to rouse her father. Then she planned to carry onward to the Tower of London to fulfil her promise to the guard who had dragged her innocent husband away. Before she could do any of that, Alicia first needed to explain the situation to Hilary's parents.

"*They did what now?*" Jonathon St. John was incensed, his face growing quite red with rage.

"Come in, come in, my dear child." Hilary's mother put her arm around Alicia's shoulder and ushered her into the sitting room like she was some wretched street urchin in need of respite from the cruel January chill. There, a fire, freshly stoked by one of the St. John's maids, crackled and danced in the brick fireplace to lend the room its warmth.

"They arrested Hilary, Dr. St. John," Alicia repeated herself, entirely forgetting her father-in-law's wish she address him as Jonathon, or even as Father. "Those dreadful men hauled my husband off into the night like he was some common criminal."

"Oh my," Sarah St. John said with a sad sigh as she sat Alicia down in the leather armchair closest to the fire. "What on earth did they do such a thing for?"

"The guard said something about treason," Alicia told her. "I'm positive it is all just some beastly mix-up, Sarah, do try not to worry."

"Mix-up indeed," the doctor grunted. "I'll give them a mix-up. How dare they break down my son's door and drag him from his bed in the middle of the night? I'll have someone's neck stretched for this!"

"What will become of our boy, Jonathon?" Sarah asked. She was, by this time, quite tearful, and Alicia found herself having to turn the tables to console her mother-in-law.

"He will be perfectly fine," Jonathon snapped, perhaps a little too brusquely. "Our son has done nothing wrong, and the St. Johns are an upstanding family in London circles. To even suggest he could be capable of anything close to approaching treason against his king and country is absolute balderdash!"

"Johnathon!" Even through her tearful grief, Sarah couldn't help but reprimand her husband's impropriety. "Not in front of the girl!" She smiled an apology at Alicia, who found the whole thing absurdly amusing, not least of which that her in-laws still referred to her as *the girl*.

"Do not mind my sensibilities, Dr. St. John. I'd say those are the least of our worries at this particular moment in time." Alicia laid a hand gently upon Sarah's shoulder by means of comfort. Alicia wished to reassure her she was not at all offended by the doctor's uncharacteristic outburst of foul language.

"We must make haste to the Tower!" Jonathan declared. "And on the way, I should call in on the king's physicians—surely they will be in a position to shed some light upon this ridiculous farce!"

"With respect, sir." Alicia had learned quickly during her association with the St. Johns playing the subordinate was by far the best way to gain both Jonathon's ear and his acquiescence. "My father is a man of the law—surely he will be better placed to navigate through the machinations of whatever laws the palace may have invoked to bring about Hilary's incarceration? However, your kind offer to visit with the palace physicians is most appreciated."

Jonathon made as if to protest but was prevented from doing so by his wife's intervention. "I think that's a sensible solution all round, Johnathon, dear." Sarah's voice wobbled as she spoke. Alicia couldn't help but admire the brave face the woman was putting on, and for the first time in their association, she saw Sarah St. John as much more than the timid, mousey doctor's wife who dwelled in her husband's shadow. "You have often said yourself how formidable a barrister Dudley Bartlett is, and how magistrates the length and breadth of London quake at the very mention of the man's name."

The doctor's nod was barely perceptible, and Alicia fancied she saw the man deflate a little. "I suppose it wouldn't hurt us to all play to our strengths in this time of adversity," he relented with a frown that crinkled his brow. "What matters here is that we liberate our son from the clutches of the establishment. Such is its incompetence under the current imbecilic rule that I have known of many a good man imprisoned—or worse—on trumped-up charges or due to ineptitude."

Alicia cringed at her father-in-law's words. He didn't have to even utter the word for her to understand his meaning behind *or worse.* Even fine, upstanding, and ultimately innocent subjects of the king had been known to take the short, one-way walk to meet with the hangman at Tyburn. That her precious husband might suffer the same fate was simply too horrible for her to contemplate.

"I am in need of a horse," Alicia blurted out. It was, after all, the main reason she had journeyed to the St. John's house, other than to deliver the dreadful news about their beloved son, of course.

"I shall instruct the stable boy to saddle up the chestnut gelding forthwith!" Jonathon was quickly back to his slightly over-important self. "He is our fastest beast by a long chalk—the sooner you get to your father and the Tower, the better. Sarah and I will remain here and await news of Hilary. I think he would be best served by a man of the law right now, and I fear Sarah does not have the fortitude to see our son in such a place as the Tower—it would break the poor woman's heart."

"Thank you *so* much," Alicia fought the urge to hug the man. Jonathon St. John was not one for being demonstrative, and she would have hated to offend him. Instead, she wrapped her arms about Sarah's neck and gave her a fond squeeze. "I promise we will have Hilary home before sunset," she whispered into Sarah's ear. "Not even the King of England himself will be a match for all of us if we pull together!"

As Jonathon strode from the room with purpose, Alicia extricated herself from his good lady wife and followed him through the kitchens and out to the stables. She had to practically trot to keep up with the doctor, who had a phenomenal pace to his step for a man of his age. All the while, Alicia was wondering how on earth she was going to explain any of this to her own mother and father.

Chapter Nine

Naturally, Dudley Bartlett, being a prominent barrister within London's legal circles, was infuriatingly pragmatic about the whole affair. He listened with patience as Alicia sobbed her way through relating what had transpired the previous night and hadn't batted so much as an eyelid at her mention of the ridiculous charges against Hilary.

"This happens more often than you'd care to believe, my dear," Dudley told her, as if that revelation would go some way towards comforting his distraught daughter. Alicia had allowed herself the luxury of breaking down into tears behind the brave façade she had maintained for the St. Johns—it wasn't as if her wonderful parents had not seen her cry a thousand times before.

"False charges and accusations run rife within the upper echelons of the palace and Whitehall. It is thanks to many of them that I have grown quite rich."

It was meant as a joke, but neither Alicia nor her mother saw any humour in it.

"And what becomes of the ill-accused?" Alicia asked, fearing the answer. "Does justice prevail, and the innocent are set free?"

Dudley's brief pause spoke volumes. "Of course, they are, my dear daughter. This is England, we practically invented *justice*!" His lie fell on stony ground.

"What will become of Hilary should justice not see good sense, Father?" Alicia asked hoarsely. Suddenly her throat felt very dry. Alicia dreaded the reply she knew in her heart lay upon the tip of her father's tongue, but she had to hear the truth, no matter how harsh it may be.

"Now, now, we must not talk that way," Dorothea fussed as she poured out three huge, steaming cups of tea from her favourite teapot—its intricately painted pattern depicted a trio of rural scenes from Northumbria. "This is all one big, silly misunderstanding, and I'm sure your father will have it all straightened out before teatime."

"It may take even I a little longer than that, my darling," Dudley ventured.

Dorothea shot her husband a withering look and then cast a fleeting glance at Alicia. "Not in front of . . ."

Alicia rolled her eyes. If her mother were to finish that sentence with *the girl* instead of a loaded silence, she might just have screamed.

"Alicia is a grown, married woman, Dorothea," Dudley chastised his wife. "She is perfectly capable of facing the difficult facts of life—especially in matters pertaining to her husband."

Alicia was grateful to her father for not treating her like some tragically delicate creature—pretty much as he and Mother had done her entire life. But she secretly wished on this occasion he might have flowered things up for her, lied even. "He's right, Mother." Alicia grasped Dorothea's hand and gave her a reassuring smile. "If I am to deal with this . . . unfortunate turn of events, I do need to know *everything* and anything that may help my poor Hilary. Please, don't fret about me. I'll be perfectly fine—and we do all need to be strong together."

Dorothea patted her daughter's hand. "Very well, Alicia." She forced herself to return the smile. "If you can be that strong, then so can I. Does anyone want scones?"

"Scones for breakfast?" Oliver's unexpected voice had his parents and sister all but jumping out of their respective skins. "What's the occasion?" He strode into the room in all his evening finery, which did appear somewhat crumpled and askew.

"Where have you been, my boy?" Bristling, Dudley demanded to know.

"At Bunny Featherstone's New Year shindig." Had Oliver rolled his eyes any harder, they may well have fallen straight from their sockets. "I *did* tell you."

"That was two days ago, my lad." Dudley puffed out his barrel chest, as he was wont to do when his son had his dander up.

"Indeed," Oliver tipped Alicia a wink, "Bunny does know how to throw one dandy of a house party. And, dear Father, I am not a young whippersnapper any longer—my comings and goings really ought not concern you." He chuckled and poured himself a cup of tea.

"Hilary was arrested." The words tumbled from Alicia's lips before she even knew what she was saying. Her only thought was to put a stop to her brother's altercation with Father before it escalated any further. That Oliver remained unwed—and thus unlikely to be providing an heir any time soon—was a constant bone of contention between the two.

"I beg your pardon?" Oliver stared at his sister as if she had gone quite mad. In his shock, he continued to pour his tea until the cup overflowed into the powder blue porcelain saucer. "Did you just say . . .?"

Alicia nodded. "Last night. The Royal Horse Guards burst into our home and took him away."

"Why, the old sea dog," Oliver grinned. "I didn't know he had it in him."

"Oliver!" Dorothea barked at her son, her eyes flashing with admonishment. "This is no laughing matter."

"But, Mother, Hilary *can* be quite the dull fellow, despite his love of boxing—I'm sure there's a perfectly reasonable explanation for his arrest."

"He is accused of treason, Oliver," Alicia said quietly, firmly. "They are holding him in the Tower."

The smile evaporated from Oliver's face in an instant. Placing the teapot back down upon the table, he embraced his sister. "I am so sorry for my careless remarks, Alicia," he whispered. "Is there anything I can do to help?"

"Just be there for me," Alicia implored.

Oliver made his promise to his dear sister. Alicia knew that, even above her unwavering parents, her brother would be a pillar of strength whenever she needed it.

"We are going to the Tower forthwith," Dudley informed his son. "Even if we are unable to have Hilary freed immediately, at least we ought to be able to see him."

"I shall have the carriage readied straight away," Oliver said. "I will make sure the stables harness our fastest horses." With that, he turned on his heels and made his way from the room.

"Thank you, Oliver!" Alicia called after him.

Oliver waved a hand over his head by means of acknowledgement and then was gone.

As things transpired, Oliver elected to stay home. He was bone-weary from his New Year revelling with Bunny and his disreputable cohorts. But more importantly, he knew he would have very little to offer at the Tower of London other than a disruptive element and perhaps his fists—both of which would be counterproductive given the circumstances.

Alicia and her parents rode in silence all the way into the city. On the way, they took a small detour to Whitechapel to call in on Gregory Sedgewick, who was as confounded as they all were at his good friend and colleague's odd predicament. It was the first time that Alicia had seen the young doctor's digs, which were in the attic of an old, disintegrating terraced house. She considered them far too cramped and dingy, and certainly not befitting of one in the medical profession, let alone one who dealt directly with the king.

"You must allow me to come along with you," Gregory insisted.

"Oh, I couldn't possibly expect that of you," Alicia told him. "I wouldn't wish to impose."

"Hilary is my good friend, Alicia," Gregory said with that crooked smile of his. "There may be something I can do, or some opinion I can sway—King George considers me one of his favourites, don't you know?"

Alicia couldn't help but give the man a thin smile. Indeed, he had regaled her at length during their pre-Christmastide tea with stories of how both the king and his simpleton son simply thought the world of Gregory, their young physician. "I am sure Hilary would love to see you," she said as she followed him down the steep wooden stairs.

"Will we get to see him?" Gregory addressed his question to Dudley as he clambered into the carriage.

Dudley huffed a little. "I should jolly well hope we do, young man," he replied with conviction. "I don't expect to have to go through the magistrates to sort through this bally mess!"

"Dudley!" Dorothea snapped. "Watch your language—*please*!"

"Sorry, dear," Dudley appeared suitably rebuked, his face turning a rather odd shade of crimson.

"You must forgive my husband's disgusting language," Dorothea apologised to Gregory. "Some days, one might think he worked at Billingsgate Wharf, and not the highest court of the land."

Alicia smirked at her mother. The woman's vehement dislike of the fish markets was a constant source of amusement; Billingsgate was pretty much her default reference for all things vulgar.

"There really is no need to apologise, Mrs. Bartlett," Gregory replied with a friendly grin. "These are indeed extraordinary times, and besides which, I can assure you I have heard far worse from our very monarch himself!"

Alicia thought that seemed to placate her mother rather well. That her barrister husband's potty mouth was on a par with that of King George may well be something for her to actually be proud of!

Around them, the early morning streets of London were springing to life. People meandered to their places of work, urchins took up their street corners with tiny bare feet already blue from the winter's chill, and drunkards lurched out from the gin palaces to seek out a little fresh air and perhaps beg something to put into their bellies other than alcohol. The bare branches of the rattling, skeletal trees lining the streets were decorated with thick frost that would take 'til noon to melt.

"It is important you leave me to do all the talking—they will listen to me as a man of the law," Dudley said as the Tower loomed up ahead. It was a tall, square, imposing building with a spiked turret at each of its corners and a forbidding wall all the way around its periphery. The Tower's infamously bloody past was all too well-known to every Londoner, as, throughout history, many noblemen, heretics, and traitors had met a grisly end within the confines of those beige stone walls. Although torture had been outlawed over a hundred years before, just the mere mention of the Tower's name was enough to send the icy chill of terror into even the stoutest of hearts.

Alicia had some misgivings about turning up mob-handed at the Tower. They were misgivings that were founded once she, Gregory, her mother, and father approached the gatehouse and demanded to see the yeoman in charge.

"He ain't available," the yeoman at the gatehouse informed Dudley Bartlett.

"I am a barrister at the London courts, and this fellow here is one of the king's physicians, as is my son. I demand you fetch your captain."

"I don't care if you're the queen of Prussia," the Yeoman sneered through crooked yellow teeth.

"May we at least see my husband?" Alicia stood forward, despite her father's earlier instructions.

The yeoman took his time to look Alicia up and down, which made her feel most uncomfortable. He was an elderly, stout chap with a thick bush of white whiskers, which had shed all down his red uniform like he was some mangy old dog. His eyes were scrunched up and rheumy, and the bulbous end of his nose had the bright redness of one who imbibed a little too much gin in his off-duty hours. Nonetheless, the yeoman was steadfast in his refusal.

"No," he said. "You may not."

"Now listen here, my good man." Alicia just couldn't help herself—the infernal yeoman of the guard had her hackles rising and seemed singularly unimpressed at her father's standing. Perhaps an emotional plea from the prisoner's poor, distraught wife may do the trick? As she spoke, Alicia studied the old man's eyes for any spark of humanity beneath his wild, voluminous eyebrows and weary lids. Sadly, she found nothing of the sort. "My husband has been falsely imprisoned here, and I have a right to see him!"

The yeoman coughed, hawked, and spat a wad of thick phlegm onto the ground by Alicia's feet. "If he's here, it's for treason," he grunted at her. "Not too long ago, his treacherous head would be stuck on a pike at Traitor's Gate by now. As it is, he'll most likely hang for his crimes—whatever they may be." The unpleasant old man seemed to take great delight in seeing Alicia cringe at such a heartless comment.

"If you would please bring your captain to the gatehouse—" Dudley insisted.

"I will do no such thing, sir," the yeoman snapped. "Now, I suggest you all be on your way before you join your treacherous son in the dungeons."

Alicia made as if to speak again—surely, she could get the awful man to see reason by using her feminine wiles. She began to cry. "Please, sir," she sobbed, "we have only been married a short time, and I miss him so." Proud of her performance, Alicia did everything short of swooning into a dead faint at the old codger's highly polished boots.

"Your tears ain't going to work on me, young miss," the old guard said. A wry smile cracked his crinkled lips beneath that seemingly impenetrable beard. "I've heard it all—seen it all, too. Be on your way, the lot of you. I have the ravens to feed." And, with that, he turned his back on the forlorn Alicia and her party and closed the heavy, wooden gatehouse door behind him.

"Ravens indeed," Dudley scoffed. "With the state of the crown these days, I'd be surprised if the Beefeaters have any of the darned birds left to take care of at all."

Alicia remained silent as the four walked with heavy hearts back to the carriage. In another time, another circumstance, her father would undoubtedly have gone on at length about how the yeomen were known as Beefeaters because they received part of their salary in beef. Legend had it that the presence of ravens at the Tower of London signified the strength of the English monarchy. Should the sinister black birds fly away, the monarchy would fall.

Of course, the Tower's ravens all had their wings clipped to prevent such an occurrence, which Alicia thought to be most cruel and wholly unnecessary in such modern, more enlightened times.

"You must come back home with us, my dear Alicia." Dorothea broke her silence. She had taken her husband's instruction to allow him to deal with matters alone to heart—after all, she was only there to support her daughter.

"That is a splendid idea," Dudley chipped in. "I will be in my chambers penning letters to the magistrates and demanding they sign for Hilary's release with immediate effect, and rather fear I will not be home much before the witching hour."

Glancing at Gregory for a little moral support, Alicia shook her head and said, "I shall return to my own house, but thank you, Mother. I would hate for Hilary to come home to an empty home upon his release, which I am confident will be very soon. Were I not there waiting for him, he may assume I think him guilty of whatever crimes he is accused of."

"Stuff and nonsense!" Dorothea huffed as she got into the chaise. Dudley and Gregory had chivalrously pulled open the door and stepped aside to allow the ladies to climb in first. At the front of the carriage, the grey stallions stomped their feet with impatience and snorted dense plumes of white breath into the chilly London air.

"Your mother is quite right, Alicia," Gregory declared. "No one in their right mind would think for even a moment Dr. Hilary St John could be guilty of anything so scandalous as treason. I consider I know him better than most, and there is no doubt at all he loves his king and country. Why else would he dedicate his life and career to finding a cure for King George against such overwhelming odds?"

"Thank you, Gregory." Dorothea seemed delighted to have found an ally against her daughter's stubbornness.

"However," Gregory went on. "I would venture to say my dear friend would prefer to not return to a cold, empty house when the Royal Horse Guards discover their terrible error."

Dorothea visibly deflated at Gregory's declaration. Still, she held her tongue—the woman knew when she was beaten. Alicia mouthed a grateful *thank you* to her husband's dear friend while her mother wasn't looking. Over and above her wish to be home to welcome Hilary back, she simply wanted to be alone.

Chapter Ten

The cottage seemed so big and empty without Hilary to fill it with his chatter and laughter. As accustomed as Alicia was to spending much of her time there alone while her husband worked, just the fact she couldn't look forward to him coming home made their home cold and lonely. Even on the occasions Hilary finally arrived home late from the city exhausted and wanting nothing more than to sleep, he would always make time to enjoy a little supper with his wife and tell her about his day.

This was to be the first time Alicia would be spending a night alone since she and Hilary had become man and wife—not counting the previous half night when the Royal Guards had so unceremoniously broken down the door and carted her husband off.

Pottering about her kitchen, Alicia drew very little comfort from the heat of the fire she'd built in the fireplace, nor from the broth she had warmed up on the stove in the candlelight. Actually, she had no appetite at all, but was sensible enough to know she had to eat something to keep up her strength. She would be of no use whatsoever to her husband as a weakened wreck. So, poor Alicia sat all alone at the kitchen table and absently dipped corpulent chunks of unleavened bread into the watery broth she'd made the weekend before from hambones and dried vegetables.

Without her realising it, Alicia's mind drifted away to hazy thoughts of Edmund and their carefree days picnicking by Sweetheart's Lake. Those had been much simpler times, and, considering her helpless predicament, she rather feared she might never feel that happy again.

Alicia did her level best to steer her mind away from Edmund and the saddening thoughts of just how much she missed him. Instead, she attempted to concentrate on positive thoughts of Hilary being released from the Tower once everyone realised what a huge mistake had been made. She lingered on the sweet memories of their romantic wedding, their talk of having a *huge* family together, and the idyllic Christmastide they had just shared—although the latter already felt like a lifetime ago.

But Alicia's stubborn mind refused to focus on such things. Instead, it would conjure faded, rippling images of her dearly departed Edmund, and she would imagine his voice echoing in her ears as they conversed in secret at Sweetheart's Lake. It was so vivid to her, as if she were back standing on the verdant banks chatting to Edmund as she had before marrying Hilary, whilst ducks and courting couples made their faint noises in the background.

"*No, Alicia*!" Scolding herself at the very notion of revisiting the lake, Alicia dunked her bread crust into the bowl of broth with such vigour the tepid liquid splashed out to stain her sleeve. "That is not an option at all."

Fully aware she was, in fact, talking to herself, Alicia at once wished she had given in to her husband's suggestion they take in a dog or a cat. One of Jonathon and Sarah's friends from their cribbage circle had a whole litter of sheepdog puppies simply begging for good homes, and they would not accept so much as a farthing from the good doctor or his son. It had all seemed wholly unnecessary at the time. Alicia had always seen pets as either practical accessories—herding sheep, hunting, or keeping rodents at bay, for example—or as child substitutes for older or barren couples or those creepy spinsters who took to the woods and were invariably tarred with the epithet *witches*.

Yet, sitting by herself in her all-too-quiet home in the late hours sipping on broth she neither wanted nor could taste, Alicia knew having an animal around would at least mean she wasn't talking to herself.

"Mother and Father would think me mad right now," Alicia mused. "Chatting away to myself, daydreaming about some long-deceased suitor." Despite her reticence, Alicia was forced to agree—with herself—that even hearing her own voice did bring some level of comfort.

Even so, it just wasn't the same.

Edmund would listen to her woes. Edmund would offer his usual wise advice, which would give her the strength to carry on and refuse to believe anything bad could possibly happen to Hilary. If only Edmund could be there for her, Alicia felt in her heart he would be able to make things so much better.

Unsurprisingly, the fact was not lost on Alicia that, had Edmund still been alive, she would be Mrs. Pembroke and living in London—and not sitting alone at a kitchen table in a cottage in Spitalfields.

He would be at the lake, though.

Edmund had promised he would be there whenever Alicia needed him—and she could have used his sympathetic ear and metaphysical shoulder to cry upon. Alicia needed to speak to someone that understood her heart. She had always felt that Edmund knew her too well.

"*No!*" The suddenness of her own voice resounding about the silent kitchen startled Alicia; so much so, she looked around just to make sure it had been her voice.

Finally giving up on the horribly cold broth, Alicia blew out all the candles but one in the kitchen and used that remaining light to take herself up to bed. The thought of sliding beneath the cold, stiff blankets all alone held about as much allure as the broth she'd left behind. However, Alicia was dog-tired to the point of collapse. She was sensible enough to know what she truly needed was a good night's sleep—or at least the best semblance of such she could muster.

As Alicia trudged her weary way up the stairs, all she could do was hope and pray exhaustion would be enough to keep her asleep until dawn.

Sleep came upon Alicia almost the moment her head touched the goose-down pillow some distant relative of Hilary's had given as a wedding gift. And, along with the welcome numbness of slumber came nebulous, swirling dreams of Royal Guards, sinister black horses and carriages with unyielding iron bars. She finally dreamt about glossy black ravens that hopped about on bright green grass, flapping useless wings as they tried in vain to fly. They were too stupid to realise that the very men who provided their food each day were the same who had taken away the glorious gift of flight bestowed upon them by the Good Lord.

The grass in Alicia's dream sloped gently away, down to the edge of the lake, which sat still, glassy, with nary a ripple in the dazzling spring sunshine.

They sat upon a thick, woollen blanket, Alicia and Edmund; just one young courting couple amongst many out enjoying a spring day Sunday picnic in Stepney Green Park.

"You must visit with me, Alicia," Edmund was saying, the delicate outline of his lips shimmering in the reflection from the lake's clear water. "It has been far too long."

With all her heart, there was nothing Alicia wanted more. But she forced herself to reply, "Alas, I cannot. To do so would be an act of betrayal to my husband. I won't be unfaithful to Hilary, especially so with the unfortunate fate which has befallen him."

"I am sure he would understand, Alicia." In her dream, Edmund's voice sounded soft, sweet, like *home.* "There are things you need to know, my love, things which may help you to help your husband. What man would not forgive his wife such a selfless action?"

"Please, Edmund," Alicia heard herself say. "You cannot call me that."

"But it is true." As the Edmond in her dream spoke, a mischievous smile played about the corners of his sweet mouth. "What are you, if not *my love*?"

"I am another man's wife." Alicia's protest was quite resolute. "I would ask that you respect that."

"Of course." Edmund cast his eyes down to the blanket, to the mouth-watering array of food spread out across the dream blanket. "I give my word to show your union nothing but the utmost respect,

Alicia, but only if you promise to make a trip to Sweetheart's Lake first thing in the morning—call it a pilgrimage, if you will."

Although she was experiencing nothing more than a vivid dream, and Alicia was very much aware of that fact, she felt as if she were actually *there*. The warmth of the sunshine and gentle breeze caressed her, the divine aromas wafting up from the food, the soft, urgent quacking of tiny yellow ducklings as they paddled single-file behind their ever-patient mothers . . .

Nothing had ever felt more *real* to Alicia than that dream moment.

"Yes." Alicia couldn't prevent the word from slipping from her tongue like some exotic sweetmeat. "I shall visit with you, Edmund, if only for my husband's sake.

Edmund's sweet face faded from her view, along with the park, the lake, and everything surrounding it as Alicia slipped into a deep, dreamless sleep.

Chapter Eleven

The Edmund in her dream was right; it had indeed been far too long since Alicia had set foot upon the grassy bank of Sweetheart's Lake and since she had held a conversation with her beloved Edmund.

Although it was the depth of wintertime, the grass crispy with a delicate layer of morning frost, and the trees stood naked and exposed around the edges of the park, the place still held a magical atmosphere for Alicia. As she led her horse across to the lake, Alicia thought of all the joyful times she had spent there and tried to imagine just how differently her life would have turned out had cholera not claimed poor Edmund's life.

The horse walked silently behind her. The grass held no interest for the beast as it was far too cold and brittle, and there were but a smattering of other people in the park to catch its attention. Alicia had borrowed the animal from Hilary's parents again—she had spun them some yarn about needing to visit with her father in Bethnal Green before he embarked for the city. She hated lying to the St. Johns, as they were wonderful people to their very core. But she couldn't even begin to envisage requesting the use of their finest horse to enable her to meet with the ghost of her dead fiancé . . . who just so happened to reside *in* Sweetheart's Lake!

And so, she had set off from Spitalfields at the crack of dawn and had found herself by the edge of the lake wondering what on earth one was supposed to say in such a situation.

The lake rippled gently beneath the soft caress of the chilly wind, "It's good to see you again, Alicia," Edmund said as his face shimmered into view beneath the quivering water. "I have missed you so much."

"And I, you, Edmund." Alicia glanced around. She was particularly self-conscious one or more of her fellow early birds may think it strange to see a young lady talking to the lake. There was also the danger—albeit incredibly remote—she may bump into someone who knew her or her family. Now, unquestionably, *that* would take some explaining!

"I am glad you decided to come." As Edmund spoke, his image shifted and flitted within the water as if it were about to break apart. "I have to warn you that you are in terrible danger."

"I understood this was to be about my husband." The word sounded altogether alien to Alicia—referring to her husband to the ghost of her beloved deceased fiancé felt somehow very wrong indeed.

Edmund's ethereal brow furrowed. "It concerns the *both* of you, Alicia—I would not deem to lure you here under false pretences," he told her. "And please believe me when I say I wish the fellow no ill will whatsoever. You may rest assured I have only the most honourable of intentions to my actions. I have seen how happy Hilary makes you, and that is of great comfort to me as one who loved you—and who loves you still."

"You have visited us?" Alicia was thoroughly shocked by the inference. "In our home?"

Edmund let out a light, playful laugh. "There's no need to be alarmed, my dear, sweet Alicia," he chuckled. "I have done nothing to invade your privacy—your modesty is perfectly intact. Actually, it hurts me that you think me capable of such a dastardly deed."

Alicia's face flushed scarlet red, and she was about to babble some heartfelt apology when she saw the familiar mischievous twinkle in Edmund's eyes. "You cad!" she exclaimed. "You are teasing me again!"

"This . . . *whole thing* is difficult for me to explain." Edmund spoke slowly, deliberately, as if addressing a particularly trying child. "I *feel* things more than I see them, but I do occasionally get a view of things that make very little sense to me—I rather think we ghosts have the gift of foresight, which can actually be most entertaining."

"You can see the future?" Alicia was positive that Edmund was back to teasing her again. "If so, you must know what will become of my husband."

"Regrettably, it doesn't quite work that way," Edmund told her, the sadness in his voice sincere. "I really wish it did—things would be so much more straightforward. I see snippets, fragments if you will, which are as disjointed as the individual pieces of the jigsaw puzzles John Spilsbury used to make—those are destined to become very popular over the next century or so, by the way." Edmund laughed softly at his own joke, which Alicia didn't quite grasp. "I have seen slivers of a world in which carriages move about freely *sans* horses, and people talk to one another all across the globe by means of tiny metal boxes—can you even begin to imagine such a contraption?!"

Alicia smiled and shook her head. No, she couldn't, and that was a hard fact. Perhaps she was not the crazier of the two of them. After all, she was only talking to a hallucination in a lake; Edmund was the one spouting such far-fetched nonsense.

Horseless carriages indeed!

"There is a man in York, a doctor." Edmund set aside talk of the future to get straight down to the business at hand. "He goes by the name of Alexander Beauchamp now—I'm afraid I have a blank space where his original name should be."

"He lives under a pseudonym?" Alicia asked. "Is the man a villain of some sort?"

"He was, until recently, one of the king's physicians," Edmund explained. "Until he was forced to flee London for fear of his very life. He may well hold the key to clearing Hilary's name and winning his freedom."

"What good is this chap to any of us if he's in York? And *may well*?"

"I'm afraid that's as solid as my newly acquired insight gets, my darling." Edmund sounded a tad deflated. "York is but three days away by coach. Do you think you may be up to the journey?"

"I am robust enough as you well know, Edmund." Alicia felt it necessary to defend herself, although she could not understand *why*. "But to undertake the expedition based upon the *feeling* of a . . ."

"Ghost?" Edmund smiled at her. "What else do you have but the intuition of one who loved you with every fibre of his being? I may not be able to provide you with a crystal-clear vision of your future, my darling Alicia, but I can tell you your trip to York to find the errant Doctor Beauchamp is absolutely critical if you are to ever save your husband from the gallows."

Alicia's gulp at the mention of the dreaded word was audible. "Don't ever use that word again, Edmund. *Please.*"

"Then promise me you will make haste to York?"

Edmund was correct, of course. She had nothing else to work with but his word. She still hoped they would simply let Hilary out of the Tower with an apology, or that her father would spin some legal magic to win his freedom. But what if Edmund's preternatural premonition was correct, and her husband was destined to end his life kicking and gasping at the end of a rope?

"I have no choice, do I?" Alicia was close to tears.

"You have two, Alicia, but one is not to be contemplated right now. Get yourself to York, locate Beauchamp, and find out what he knows that will help Hilary. It really is most straightforward."

"I can't possibly make that trip alone," Alicia protested. "The carriages and carriage houses are no place for a young lady travelling alone, and I couldn't possibly ask Mother."

"You are stronger than you give yourself credit for, my darling Alicia," Edmund said sternly. "I have always looked up to you and admired you. And don't forget, I will be by your side every single step of the way."

By the time Alicia walked away from Edmund, Sweetheart's Lake, and Stepney Green Park, the day was truly getting underway. Her mind was racing so rapidly she could barely catch her own thoughts to analyse what was expected of her. Was she really contemplating travelling all the way to York just because the ghost of her dead fiancé advised it? What if she *was* insane and she'd merely imagined the entire episode? They could hang Hilary before she could catch a carriage back!

But, in her heart, Alicia knew—*felt*—it was all genuine, and her treasured Edmund truly wished to help rescue her happiness. Besides, she had liked hearing him call her *darling* once again; she had missed that terribly.

Chapter Twelve

"That is far too perilous a journey for a young lady to contemplate," Gregory Sedgewick told her. "The Great North Road is fraught with danger. I hear tell that ruthless highwaymen still patrol its remote stretches, and there are plenty of those beyond St. Albans. Have you not heard of Dick Turpin?"

Alicia couldn't be sure if her husband's dear friend and colleague was fooling with her or not, as his sense of humour often bordered upon the sardonic. He had called in to visit with her for news of Hilary, of which she sadly had none. She didn't mind too much that the young man had taken it upon himself to turn up at the cottage unannounced. Truth be told, she rather welcomed Gregory's company, even if he was a tad pompous at times. There was even a part of her that wished she could share with him her conversation with Edmund, although something held her back. He was a physician, after all, and he would surely think her mad.

"They hung him almost eighty years ago, you silly goose." Alicia gave a light laugh to let Gregory know she was teasing. "And there hasn't been a report of a highwayman anywhere on the Great North Road in almost a decade now. I truly believe I will be perfectly safe on my journey."

"What on earth has possessed you, my dear Alicia?" Gregory asked as she poured out two cups of steaming black tea from the ornamental teapot her mother had given her as a housewarming gift. It had been her grandmother's and was adorned with scenic views of the crumbling shale cliffs of the Whitby coastline.

"*Possessed* me?" Alicia was somewhat taken aback by Gregory's choice of word.

"To even contemplate travelling all the way to York when poor Hilary is incarcerated in the Tower and facing a terrible fate." Gregory grimaced, as if the hangman's noose were tightening around his throat instead of his friend's. "Surely your husband will be better served were you to remain close by to comfort him in his hour of need."

Alicia shook her head and took a sip of her tea. "They will not allow me to see him, Gregory," she said with great sadness in her voice. "I doubt very much they will let anyone see him until he is put to trial. And then it will be from the public gallery at the magistrates' court. I feel my sweet, innocent Hilary will be best served by my doing absolutely everything within my powers to clear his name—not sitting here feeling sorry for myself, and certainly not by running fruitlessly back and forth to London like some poor puppy chasing a stick only to have it tossed away again."

"But why *York*, Alicia?" As Gregory took a slurp of his tea, droplets gathered upon his moustache to give the appearance of morning dew on a dark bramble bush.

Once more, Alicia contemplated telling Gregory all about Edmund, her clandestine trip to Sweetheart's Lake, and that her long-dead fiancé had insisted she take the journey north to seek out Dr. Beauchamp. But it occurred to her Gregory would likely know the man and may reveal something about him that would put her off the idea completely. Or that he might have her immediately committed to the insane asylum for all her talk of conversing with ghosts. Even taking into account her delicate state of distress at the wrongful arrest of her new husband, Alicia knew she couldn't take that risk if she was to save Hilary's neck.

"I have it on good authority I may find the answers I need there, Gregory." Alicia tried her very best not to sound too mysterious. Nonetheless, she clearly had the young man intrigued.

"May I enquire as to whom has advised you of such?" Gregory shuffled about in the hard, wooden chair and tapped his long, slender fingers upon the kitchen table.

"I'm afraid I am not at liberty to disclose that information," Alicia told him, and hoped against hope he would be satisfied with that.

However, he was not.

"You know you have my absolute confidence, Alicia," Gregory pressed with a thin smile that was all but concealed beneath his beard. "If you were to divulge your source, it would go no further than this very kitchen. Indeed, I may even know of the fellow and be in a position as to advise you upon his trustworthiness . . . or otherwise."

"Oh, you can rest assured he is trustworthy, Gregory," Alicia replied with confidence. If there was one person on the entire face of God's green earth that she knew she could trust implicitly, it was Edmund.

If only she could tell Gregory that, perhaps he would put a stop to his questioning.

"I'm sure you think so." Gregory was beginning to sound condescending, which didn't sit well with Alicia at all. "But the world is full of scoundrels and charlatans who spend their time scheming upon how best to take advantage of vulnerable young ladies such as your good self."

"What possible motivation would someone have in advising me to travel all the way to York?"

Gregory visibly recoiled at Alicia's incredulous tone. "Perhaps he—or she, for I understand women can be equally as duplicitous as men, if not more so on occasion—has reason for sending you away from London and away from Hilary."

Sipping upon her tea, which was the perfect temperature but simply begged for scones to go with it, Alicia allowed herself a moment or so to contemplate that thought. Would Edmund want her out of the way so that she could not help her husband? Could it even be possible that her dearly departed fiancé might just be jealous of Hilary for having the life with Alicia he had once dreamed of?

Shaking her head to clear away the nefarious thoughts, Alicia admonished herself; Edmund would *never* do such a thing! He was as dear and sweet and honest in death as he had been in life, and Alicia knew in her heart he was guiding her with the very best of intentions. Edmund wanted her to be happy, and he was using all the powers at his disposal to ensure Hilary's release from the Tower—even if it did mean she was going to be over two hundred miles and three days away.

"And just what might that reason be, Gregory?" The cutting edge to her voice surprised Alicia, although she hoped Gregory would take the hint and leave well alone. She'd decided against telling him about Edmund—for the time being, at least.

"Perhaps the chap owns the stagecoach company?" Gregory's attempt at humour was a clear indication he'd given up on his line of questioning—it would appear he knew a stubborn woman when he came across one. "His advice could be construed to sell another ticket—they are not to be had for a few farthings you know."

"I have the money, thank you, Gregory," Alicia reassured him.

Gregory reached out a hand across the table and grasped Alicia's. She gasped—not only at the suddenness of his action, but at the impropriety of it, too. However, she decided, given the circumstances, she would assume it was a comforting gesture and nothing more, and opted to leave her hand where it was.

"My dear Alicia," Gregory spoke softly, as if addressing a small child who had tumbled over in the street. "You are determined to make your trip to York; I can see that in your eyes. But, please, promise me you will sleep on your decision before you depart to catch the stagecoach? And, should you still be of a mind to go come morning time, I will accompany you as your chaperone to ensure the safety of my good friend's wife."

"I promise I shall sleep on it, Gregory, and I thank you for your kind offer, but—"

Gregory took his hand from Alicia's, raising it to silence her protest. "I shall hear nothing more of it, my dear," he declared with his familiar pomposity. "Should you remain unwavering in your intention to travel into the wilds of Yorkshire on the whim of some unknown benefactor, then I shall be by your side every step of the way."

"York is hardly the wilds of anywhere, Gregory," Alicia teased with a chuckle. "I hear they have water closets and everything up north nowadays."

"Yorkshire is a grim, dangerous place for we city folk." Gregory sounded stern and reminded Alicia somewhat of her father when he'd imbibed a little too much French wine over Sunday dinner.

"I have seen paintings of the countryside," she told him. "The Dales are particularly splendid, as are the Pennines, although this time of the year, they are apt to be somewhat bleak."

"Then my case is rested," Gregory stated with firmness as he stood up from his chair and made ready to leave. "We have a plan of action, depending upon your final decision in the morning."

It was getting late. Alicia was bone weary, and her head was spinning with everything Edmund had told her. She had little fortitude to argue further with Gregory, as he had quite evidently made up his mind about accompanying her to York. So, she nodded politely, showed her husband's odd friend to the door, and bid him a good night.

Chapter Thirteen

Alicia was awoken in the late hour of that night by the distinctive smell of smoke.

In the darkest depths of her dreams, the acrid tang stirred childhood memories of late summers in the countryside when the farmers would burn the stubble in the fields in preparation for the wintertime. Edmund was there with her. They walked hand-in-hand along a long, winding country road to admire the trees that were just beginning to turn into the reds and browns that heralded the arrival of autumn.

"You must wake up, Alicia," Edmund was saying to her as they meandered past a mountainous stack of hay bales by a rickety old gate. The dry straw was smouldering, the dark grey smoke spiralling up into the burnished brass sky to obscure the sun's light with a tall, dirty shadow.

"Wake up, my darling," Edmund implored with a squeeze of her hand; there was concern in his beautiful eyes. "You are in danger—now is not the time for you to be sleeping. *You must get out.*"

"Get out of where?" The words tripped from Alicia's lips as she returned to wakefulness, her head still partly immersed in the lucid dream. It had all seemed so real, and Edmund had seemed so tangible that Alicia could still feel the warm smoothness of his hand in hers.

Sitting up in her bed, Alicia held the blankets around her shoulders against the cold chill of the night air and couldn't help but shiver. Her bed was cosy and warm, and she had little desire to leave it in the middle of the night on the say so of a dream—even if it was one of Edmund.

It was then Alicia spied the flickering orange glow in the gap beneath her bedchamber door and the wispy dark shadows that broke it up like small, ghostly fingers reaching into the room, as if searching for something to caress.

Smoke.

With a jolt, Alicia was at once fully awake. All thoughts of her idyllic dream along some country lane evaporated like morning dew on a cobweb. The only vestige remaining of her slumber was of Edmund's sweetly urgent voice telling her she must *get out*.

Clambering from her bed, Alicia wrapped the counterpane about her body for warmth and ventured toward the bedchamber door. There was no need for a candle, as the eerie glow beneath the door provided illumination enough. There, Alicia paused, her heart pounding so hard in her chest she feared it may just burst out through her ribs. She rested a hand upon the doorknob and was surprised at just how warm the usually cold brass felt to the touch.

Alicia took in a deep breath and cracked open the door.

Her face was met by a blast of warm air. Her eyes assaulted by the bright oranges and yellows of the fire that was going about its ruthlessly efficient business of devouring her home with lethal intent.

She slammed the door shut, but not before thick, black tendrils of smoke forced their way in thorough the gap to claw at the back of her throat. Sputtering, Alicia backed away from the door. All thoughts of making a calm exit through it and down the stairs to the safety of the garden spun from her mind as quickly as they had appeared. To all intents and purposes, she was trapped.

The window!

Remembering that to panic in such a situation could mean the difference between life and death, Alicia calmly padded across to the other side of the room. Her bare feet were worryingly warm on the wooden floorboards. There on the oak dresser sat her washbasin and large Wedgwood china jug of water; alongside it, a neatly pressed washcloth.

Trying her best to take only shallow breaths through her button nose—she'd read the nose was an excellent filter in keeping smoke from the throat—Alicia plunged the washcloth into the jug to soak it through. The water was icy cold and prickled her fingertips. She recalled Hilary regaling her with tales of how, as a small child growing up in Spitalfields, he'd had to break through a thin crust of ice each morning in order to rinse his face.

With the water-soaked cloth pressed to her nose and mouth, Alicia found it a little easier to breathe. It was such a relief to fill her lungs with much-needed air without choking. The smoke was billowing into her bedchamber through not only the half-inch gap at the base of the door, but around the sides, too. The window really was her only choice, but how she was going to make it out from her second-storey room without breaking a bone or two, Alicia wasn't certain. Nonetheless, given her immediate predicament, snapping an ankle or a shin bone seemed a more attractive option than being burned to a crisp by the all-consuming flames.

Using the smoky glow to guide her, Alicia rushed across to the window and pulled the heavy curtains aside. Outside, the night sky was a gloomy, starless dark, interrupted only by a faint orange glimmer she knew was from her burning home.

Fumbling around in the murky darkness, Alicia's fingers located the window latch after what felt like an eternity. She flicked it aside and pushed at the heavy frame as her mind raced ahead to just how she was expected to vacate her bedchamber without so much as a convenient ledge or tree limb to climb out onto. Nonetheless, it was a welcome conundrum for her to have, since it would mean she would be away from the flames.

The window refused to budge.

"*Confound it*!" Alicia was pleased her husband was not around to witness such unladylike profanity; even despite the pickle in which she found herself, she'd shocked herself to hear such words from her own mouth.

Alicia pushed at the window with her shoulder and realised she'd never actually opened the bedchamber window before. In the summer, it would serve only to invite in a whole multitude of unpleasant flying insects and dust, and in the wintertime, it was far too cold to warrant opening.

Which meant she had no idea if the thing could open at all.

The cold grip of fear gripped Alicia as thoughts of a grim, fiery demise filled her mind, and all she could think of was that she would never see her darling Hilary again.

"Break the window, Alicia." Edmund's voice came through as clearly as if he were standing at her shoulder; so much so, Alicia spun around expecting to see him there.

All she saw was yellow-tinged darkness and smoke.

Darting back across the room, Alicia picked up the heavy jug and scurried to the window, slopping chilly water over her feet on her way. Stopping a stride or so away from the window, she hurled the jug—icy water and all—at the dead centre of the frame.

The sudden rush of cold night air through the shattered glass and splintered frame was most welcome. Alicia gulped in great, heaving breaths, which spread like ice through her body. Behind her, the bedchamber door crackled and spat as flames crawled along the wood and into the room and her bedclothes began to smoulder. It was only a matter of time before the dry wooden floor took light and then she'd be finished for sure.

The window was smashed, and its frame broken sufficiently for Alicia to make her way out of the bedchamber, but she still had no plan as to what to do next.

"*Alicia*!" The voice startled her. She looked around. For a heartbeat, she thought Edmund had returned to guide her. But no, it wasn't his voice—this one was altogether deeper, more frantic, and *real*.

Not caring if she cut her feet on the wicked shards of glass that had fallen inwards, Alicia stepped forward and peered out through the window.

There, out on the back lawn of the cottage, stood a group of villagers—a dozen or so at least, and others were emerging out of the darkness. It would appear most of Spitalfields had come to her aid. In their midst, she saw Jonathon and Sarah St. John—it was her father-in-law who had called her name, and she was a tad embarrassed she'd not recognised it.

"You will have to jump!" Mr. St. John shouted up to her. "Don't worry! We'll catch you!" He held up a large blanket, which was grasped firmly at each corner by himself, Sarah, and a couple of strapping young men from the village, who wore thick coats and boots over their night things.

"I don't think I can," Alicia called back, even as the heat from the burning door prickled the back of her neck. "Do you not have a ladder?"

"There's no time!" One of the sturdy young men shouted back, an air of exasperation in his voice.

"The downstairs ceilings are about to collapse!" Mr. St. John added. "You *really* have to jump, Alicia!"

Of course, by downstairs ceilings, her father-in-law meant the very floor upon which Alicia was standing, the boards nice and toasty warm beneath her bare soles. As she contemplated her options—of which there were worryingly few—Alicia thought she felt the floor shift a little, or it may just have been her overactive imagination. Surely, out of all of the villagers gathered below to watch her house burn, someone would be able to lay their hands on a ladder?

The cottage let out a terrible, ungodly groan and the door to Alicia's bedchamber collapsed in from its frame as the floor shuddered and bowed downwards.

As quick as a flash, Alicia threw her counterpane over the windowsill to cover the broken glass and leapt up just as the floor vanished into the inferno of the kitchen below. Then, with the fearsome heat at her back for motivation, Alicia launched herself at the blanket spread out and held taut below. She closed her eyes, and hoped for the best.

Chapter Fourteen

Dawn had barely broken when Alicia arrived at the Whitechapel coaching inn, which had the dubious honour of being named The Hangman's Rest. Alicia did her best to ignore that and refused to believe it might be a sign of terrible things to come, especially given the unpleasant events of the previous night.

Alicia's parents-in-law had insisted she stay the night with them, having accosted her the second she'd clambered off the blanket they'd used to catch her, following her wholly inelegant leap from the conflagration. Sarah St. John had been particularly thoughtful and had ushered the crying, shaking Alicia away from the cottage so she wouldn't have to bear witness to its final death throes as timbers succumbed to the flames and the stone walls crumbled inward. The fire had lit up the cold night sky well into the night, as the villagers saw no reason in risking their lives to save what was left of the cottage. As such, there really had been nothing much remaining by the time the last of them had arrived upon the scene.

Dr. St. John—Alicia still struggled with referring to him as Johnathon, no matter how often the man insisted—had insisted that Alicia be given some steaming hot chocolate upon returning to his house. As Alicia let the rich chocolate warm her, he regaled her with the most peculiar anecdote of how he and his good lady wife came to be alerted to the fire at the cottage in the middle of the night.

"It was the darndest thing," he'd told Alicia with an uncharacteristically deep frown that furrowed his brow like some early spring field. "I was sound asleep and dreaming of a fine day at the St. Leger races when I heard a voice." At that point in the retelling, the doctor poked a finger into his left ear and wiggled it about a tad as if he was hearing the phantom voice all over again.

He went on, "Loud and clear, it was. As if the young man was standing right there beside me."

"Young man?" Alicia asked.

Dr. St. John gave a firm nod. "Absolutely, and without a doubt," he declared. "It was most *definitely* a young man's voice—and I swear blind I actually felt his breath on my ear, to boot!"

"So, who was it?" Alicia wanted to know; even in her distressed state, she already had an inkling.

"Now, there's the most curious thing of all," the doctor replied, his frown deepening further still. "When I turned around to see who was addressing me in such an urgent manner, there was absolutely no one there at all." Removing the finger from his ear, Alicia's father-in-law had briefly inspected its tip, and then resumed the telling of his odd tale. "Now, I know it was all just some silly dream, but it all seemed so very *real*—I could even smell the horses' leavings in the stables!"

Wrinkling her nose at the very thought, Alicia had considered even that aroma would have been preferable to the sour stink of smoke from her ruined home that clung to the inside of her nostrils like . . . well, like a bad smell.

"And what did this disembodied young man's voice say, Dr. St. John?"

"At the time, it seemed a peculiar thing to crop up in my dream, but with hindsight, it made perfect sense," he told Alicia. "The voice told me I must go to my window and look to the southeast. Yes, he was very specific about the direction, as I recall. And, please, do call me Jonathon."

"Of course, I'm so very sorry," Alicia apologised sweetly, although she knew she'd probably never be able to keep it up.

"Now, I'm not a superstitious man, nor am I of a religious inclination, as you well know," Jonathon preempted the peculiar part of his story with his characteristic gravitas. Alicia knew the man well enough to know he had little time for the church and all its machinations, and he only ever attended each Sunday upon the insistence of his wife. Having said that, though, Alicia had sensed a slight crumbling of the man's resolve as his story went on. "Upon awakening more abruptly than I'd have liked, I indulged the voice I'd heard in my dream and took a peek out of my bedchamber window . . ."

Alicia was sure her father-in-law was deliberately building up his part, which she hadn't found at all endearing considering the fact she'd lost her home and almost her life. Nonetheless, she sipped at the warm, soothing hot chocolate, and listened.

"Upon looking to the southeast, I saw the faintest orange glow lighting up the dark sky," the doctor said with hushed reverence. "And immediately, I knew you were in danger. I had no way of knowing for sure it was your house that was on fire, but yet I *did* know. And, of course, I was somewhat tragically proven right. Just how peculiar is that, my dear girl?"

Alicia agreed with him it was an unbelievable set of circumstances that had resulted in the St. Johns rousing half the village to rush to her aid. Indeed, had it not been for the doctor's dream and the mysterious voice therein, she might well have not been around to listen to what, ostensibly, appeared to be a tall tale.

Naturally, Sarah chalked the whole thing up to God looking out for her daughter-in-law. He had visited with Jonathon in his dream—albeit a dream involving the particularly wicked pastime of gambling—to alert him to Alicia's peril. Funnily enough, Sarah noted the good doctor had not actually argued with her, as was his wont whenever she credited God with good happenings.

"Whoever your mysterious dream voice was, I'm delighted he caught your attention," Alicia replied after what she considered to be an acceptable period of contemplation. She knew, of course, it had been Edmund. Who else *could* it have been? Alicia was not a great believer in coincidences, especially ones as specific as Dr. St. John's, and since her conversation with Edmund at Sweetheart's Lake following Hilary's arrest, backed up by her lucid dream that night in which

Edmund had roused her from her slumber, she was apt to believe he'd had a hand in alerting Dr. St. John. She really had little idea of the rules and regulations surrounding visitations from the netherworld, or wherever it was her dear Edmund resided in death. Perhaps he'd known she would require help in escaping the inferno. Had it not been for Sarah and Jonathon rallying the villagers and thinking of the clever blanket idea, she may well have been well on her way to joining Edmund in the afterlife. Alicia would be eternally grateful for her departed fiancé's intervention that terrible night. Because of him, she was alive and well to seek justice for Hilary, and she was on her way to York.

It was a bitterly cold morning. An icy sou'wester was blowing in off the Thames, bringing with it the all-too-familiar reek of the gallons of human waste the good citizens of London poured into the river on a daily basis. It had been such a long time since anyone had seen so much as a minnow in the murky brown water. There was a great deal of speculation there may never have ever been fish in the river at all! Alicia pulled her tartan shawl about her shoulders and shivered against the chill. The thick Scottish wool afforded some comfort against the winter air, but still her feet were like ice blocks in her boots.

Alicia was travelling light, having lost everything but the nightclothes she'd leapt from her bedchamber window in to escape the cruel, all-consuming fire. Sarah had donated some clothes for the journey, which she had packed neatly into the dark-tan leather valise with her typical efficiency. The clothes consisted mainly of plain, pale-blue dresses, lace bonnets, and modest undergarments. Alicia had accepted the clothes with a gracious thank you and made up her mind on the spot to purchase new upon her arrival in York and a trip to the bank. The small amount of money Dr. St. John had given her wouldn't last far beyond paying for food on the way and tipping the driver. She'd heard the dress shops in the city were of the finest quality and was quite excited at the prospect.

Had Sarah St. John been concerned about her daughter-in-law travelling to what she considered to be the wild, lawless lands of Northern England, she had no reason to worry herself. Gregory Sedgewick arrived at the coaching inn with a valise of his own in hand.

He'd turned up shortly after the St. Johns and Alicia had alighted the doctor's chaise and tethered the horses by the inn's water troughs.

"I had a feeling you'd not be deterred from taking your journey," Gregory told Alicia with a wink. "You are a woman of incredibly strong will—I could see that from the very first moment Hilary introduced us."

"I did consider your advice and warnings," Alicia lied to the young man. "But I must do what I feel is right in order to help my husband—I gave a promise to myself I would stop at nothing until he is freed."

"And I admire your fortitude, my dear," Gregory replied with a wide smile beneath his beard, which Alicia thought looked to have been trimmed and tidied a touch since the day before. "And I, being a man of *my* word, am to accompany you upon your adventure to ensure your safe passage and return for my good friend and colleague, Hilary."

Whilst Alicia felt a little irritated at Gregory taking it upon himself to assume she was not capable of taking care of her own well-being for a few days, she was nevertheless pleased at the thought of having company for the long, arduous trip. With everything she had been through of late, Alicia hadn't really relished such a protracted period with only her own sad thoughts to keep her entertained.

"We are delighted you will be going along," Sarah St. John gushed at Gregory, as her husband gave him a hearty handshake. "Our dear daughter-in-law will need a good, strong man by her side when she gets to the north." Sarah visibly shuddered as if at the very thought of a genteel young city woman being at the mercy of the horrible northern heathens. Alicia thought it most amusing, especially so as she was entirely confident she was capable of taking care of herself and that she had Edmund by her side, although he had yet to make his presence clear that morning.

"I can assure you no harm whatsoever will come to her." Gregory beamed as he planted a light, bristly kiss upon the back of Mrs. St. John's hand. "I am prepared to defend Hilary's wife as if she was my very own—I will even give my life should it be necessary to do so."

"I really do hope it won't come to that." Sarah looked even more worried than before.

"As do I, Mrs. St. John." Gregory played up his part of the gallant young hero with aplomb, and Sarah was fairly lapping it up.

"Come, now, Gregory," Alicia urged, taking her cue from the rotund, surly coach driver who made an exaggerated show of looking at his fob watch; it was evidently time to go.

Gregory clambered into the carriage after Alicia and pulled the door closed behind him. Alicia leaned out through the open widow to bid her husband's parents farewell and so they could tell her *bon voyage*. How she wished her own parents could have been there to see her off, even Oliver would have been a welcome face on that cold, bleak morning. But she had decided against telling them of her intended travels, and of the fire; she knew they would only worry. Dr. St. John had promised he would break the news once she was well on her way to York, and thus relieved Alicia of the extra anxiety of having to deal with her fraught parents.

With a click of the tongue and gentle tap with the reins, the carriage driver had the four magnificent chestnut mares clip-clopping away from the Hangman's Rest and the Doctor and Mrs. St. John. Alicia waved until they were out of sight, then closed the carriage window and settled down for the long journey north.

Chapter Fifteen

It was nightfall on the third day of travelling when York's magnificent Roman walls came into view. It was a dour, miserably cold day, which was quite typical for the north in the depths of winter. Alicia peered out through the carriage window and shivered; she was going to need much more than a woollen shawl to keep herself warm.

The journey had been quite uneventful, despite two overnight stays in less than respectable coaching inns along the way—the Napping Dragon and the somewhat worryingly named Turpin's Nag. The food at both had been adequate and refreshingly cheap, and although Alicia had chosen not to partake, the ale was supposedly fine, too. If for nothing more than those two nights alone, Alicia had been grateful for Gregory's presence. Knowing he was in the room adjacent to hers brought some comfort in the late hours as the inn's patrons grew ever rowdier in direct proportion to the seemingly endless amounts of ale they consumed. Eventually, one by one, they fell silent in their respective drunken stupors—some not even making it back to their rooms.

The rooms had been barely adequate—not enough room to swing a cat, as her father would have so eloquently put it. Still, in each there was a bed with a comfortable straw-filled mattress and a perfunctory nightstand, upon which stood a washbasin and jug of freshly drawn well water. Alicia had slept surprisingly soundly on both nights; she put that down to the long hours and mind-numbing boredom of the journey. Her books had all burned along with her home, and Sarah St. John had packed only a Bible for reading material—oh how she craved the company of Elizabeth Bennet, John Thorpe, or the Dashwood Sisters!

Unfortunately, Alicia's travelling companions were not much help by the way of alleviating the tediousness of the long, straight road. Gregory did his level best to entertain with witty chitchat, lively anecdotes of his days as a young doctor about town, and life within the palace walls. But even he ran out of things to say after a day and a half, and Alicia feared the poor fellow became as terminally bored as herself.

There were the Balfours—a splendid elderly couple who were escaping cholera-stricken London for their life of retirement in a tiny village called Holmfirth, which sat on the very edge of the Yorkshire Moors. There was also a handsome, mysterious young gentleman who deftly avoided all attempts by Alicia to divulge his profession or his purpose in visiting the walled city. He did have the most intriguing accent, though, which put Alicia in mind of something vaguely Eastern European or perhaps even South African—it was difficult to ascertain, since he spoke very little throughout the entire three-day journey.

And that was it, which was why she'd never been so pleased to see a Roman wall in her entire life!

As the carriage driver skilfully manoeuvred the chaise through the narrow Micklegate Bar entrance and into the cobbled streets of the city, Alicia worried he might scrape the shiny black sides of the vehicle. But the man had obviously made the trip more than enough times to trot the horses through with inches to spare on either side.

"It looks like we're here," Gregory announced with a relieved sigh. He stretched out his arms and cracked his neck, as if he'd awoken from a deep slumber.

"I dare say that we are, young man." Mr. Balfour humoured Gregory with a friendly smile. He and his wife were far from the end of their journey—they were to rest overnight before catching another coach early the next morning to Scarborough, and from there, yet another to their final, idyllic destination.

As for the other gentleman, it maddened Alicia she had not even managed to learn his full name. He'd asked her to call him *Sir James* and he slipped surreptitiously out into the night the moment the carriage rolled to a halt outside the tiny guesthouse in which Alicia and Gregory were to stay while in York.

So perplexing was the enigmatic Sir James, it wasn't until quite some time later, as Alicia and Gregory relaxed over a light supper of bread and pickles that something occurred to her.

"He didn't have any luggage." Alicia broke what had been a long, contemplative silence between herself and Gregory.

"Who didn't?" Gregory was bone weary and ready for his bed instead of the dining room of Widow Atkinson's guesthouse, which was so small it could only just contain the pair of wobbly old tables and half a dozen mismatched chairs. Cozy, Alicia had called it, while Gregory had opted for the more apt cramped.

"The young gentleman." Alicia rolled her eyes at her companion. "When he left the stagecoach, he didn't stop to collect any luggage from the roof. Why, the driver hadn't even had time to get down from his seat before the chap raced off. I doubt if he even tipped the poor man."

"We were supposed to tip the driver?" Gregory teased.

"Of course," Alicia told him. "Just because we are no longer in London, it doesn't mean we can behave like savages. I gave the driver a shilling and two farthings for his trouble—he did get us all the way to York safely, after all."

"I wish I could be paid a shilling and two farthings on top of my wages just for sitting on my rump!" Gregory laughed out loud and took a swig of the ale Widow Atkins had served up with the fresh-baked, warm crusty bread.

Embarrassed at the raucous guffaw, Alicia glanced around. They were entirely alone in the dining room, as the Balfours had retired early to bed in preparation for their early start and another long leg of their adventure. "That poor driver sat on his rump for three days!" Alicia blushed a little at using the word; it was hardly ladylike, and certainly not becoming of a young doctor's wife. "*Three days*, Gregory, in the bitter cold and rain, and with nary a complaint."

"He was hardly a jolly fellow," Gregory countered.

"Would you be jolly if you had his job?" Alicia laughed. "I was surprised he dismounted his seat with such agility after such a gruelling expedition. Had that been me, I think I would have remained frozen there until someone carried me away."

Gregory laughed along at the very thought, and the two relaxed for the first time in several days. For the briefest of moments, all thoughts of Hilary's cruel predicament, Mad King George, the burned cottage, and everyone she'd left behind two hundred miles away faded just enough for Alicia to embrace the feeling she was doing something truly monumental in her life.

Chapter Sixteen

York, England. 1820

The next day was one filled with surprises for Alicia.

She awoke in her modest bedchamber to the sounds of the hawkers on the street below announcing their wares to the early morning passers-by. Widow Atkinson's guesthouse was situated about a third way along The Shambles, which, from what she had seen of it the night before, Alicia considered to be a somewhat quaint little cobbled street in the centre of the city—that it was within sight of the colossal York Minster with its gothic handcrafted stone and stained-glass windows was quite the bonus!

The street had, once upon a time, been entirely populated by butcher shops, although only a handful remained. It had been known as The Great Flesh Shambles way back in the fourteenth century, which made Alicia's skin crawl just a little. In fact, the guesthouse itself had once been such an establishment, and some of the original meat hooks still hung from the ceilings. Alicia was convinced she'd been able to make out ancient bloodstains on the rough walls of the dining room the evening before.

Alicia's first surprise of that morning was, upon opening the curtains covering the tiny window of her bedchamber, discovering just how close the upper window of the building opposite hers was. She'd seen lithographs and paintings of the street before, of course, and had glanced up at the twin rows of adorable, overhanging, timber-framed structures upon arrival at The Shambles, but she'd had no concept of the nearness of the opposing windows.

As it was, Alicia was astounded to find that the thick-paned glass squares of her window to be mere inches away from those of the room opposite. The room was occupied by a rather handsome gentleman of more mature years than herself. The man offered her a warm smile upon noticing her staring in at his room. Blushing slightly, Alicia gave a wave of the hand and a cordial smile.

Breakfast was a simple affair with the rather plump, squat, plain-of-face Widow Atkinson fussing over Alicia and Gregory as if they were the only guests she'd had in a long while. Alicia believed the cholera epidemic may well have put paid to many visitors to York—one way or another. For as simple as it was, Widow Atkinson's breakfast fayre was splendidly delicious. The wonderful aroma of fresh, home-baked honey cake, saffron, and ginger filled the minuscule dining room, which made for a most welcome greeting.

"I was up at th' crack of dawn to bake for Mr. and Mrs. Balfort," Widow Atkinson explained as she served Alicia and Gregory a cup each of steaming hot chocolate—it was quite the Dandy's breakfast! "Couldn't see those good folks off wi'out a proper breakfast inside 'em."

And that was Alicia's second surprise. She had been brought up to believe that the north was filled with heathens and scoundrels, but these were warmhearted, kindly people who just happened to talk funny. So much so that Alicia was having a hard time following what Widow Atkinson was saying. She had begun to wonder if the keepers of the Yorkshire dialect had deliberately opted to omit the letter "h" altogether!

"That's awfully nice of you," Alicia said with a smile. It had only been by a sheer stroke of luck she'd caught up with the elderly Balfours on their way out of the guesthouse to embark on the next leg of their epic journey. Alicia had wished them both *bon voyage* and good health and waved them off from the guesthouse door. She was surprised at herself for feeling so very sad in knowing she would unlikely see the Balfours again. Perhaps journeying with people brought with it a camaraderie she hadn't been party to?

"Ah'll bring out th' bread and cheese in a bit," the widow interrupted Alicia's reverie.

"That won't be necessary," Gregory said. "Mrs. St. John and I have an early start and a long day, and I'd hate for us to be weighed down with bellies full of your wonderful cooking." He'd turned on the Sedgewick charm, which had the old widow giggling like a cheeky schoolgirl.

"Why, Mr. Sedgewick," Widow Atkinson grinned, "you're too kind."

"We shall be back for teatime, though," Alicia added. "And I'll warrant we will both have worked up quite the appetite by then!"

"Liver and onions for tea," the widow said as she stepped away from the table to allow her guests to eat in peace. "Perhaps a kidney, too, if I can get a couple from yon butcher before they're all gone." She pointed a long, bony finger to the shop front clearly visible through the dining room window. There, standing amongst the array of pig and sheep carcasses and myriad cuts of fresh meat, stood the gentleman with whom Alicia had exchanged a particularly unorthodox good morning.

Alicia averted her eyes.

"Embarrassed?" Edmund's sweet, teasing voice came out of nowhere. Startled, Alicia only just managed to stop herself turning around to look for him. "And so you should be for flirting with such unseemly thoughts—and you a respectable married woman and all!"

"Are you all right, Alicia?" Gregory looked most concerned at Alicia's sudden change of countenance. "I do hope you're not sickening for something."

Alicia shook her head with such vigour she feared her bonnet may slip down and cover her eyes—it appeared as though her mother-in-law was of a rather larger circumference of the head than she. "I'm perfectly fine, thank you," she assured her companion. "I think the enormity of the task ahead has me a little overwhelmed—that's all." She took a long, welcome sip of her hot chocolate, which warmed her belly and brought comfort all at the same time. Growing up, chocolate had always been her mother's drink of choice. She thought it was perfect for easing sickness and soothing the inevitable bumps and bruises of childhood. And, as Alicia and Oliver had reached that certain age, for helping mend broken hearts.

"Well, we are here now," Gregory said with a heavy sigh. "And I'm pleased to see I'm not the only one wondering just what the dickens we are supposed to do if we are to find the answers you so desperately seek."

"There is a fellow we must locate—and with some urgency, of course." Alicia looked Gregory in the eye. He must have thought her quite mad, but she was grateful the man was gracious enough to humour her.

"Of course," Gregory agreed. "But who is this fellow? And how on earth are we to find him in a city of thousands—a city of which neither of us have any knowledge whatsoever." Taking a huge bite out of the thick slab of honey cake Widow Atkinson had cut for him, Gregory continued, "Of course, you have no idea what this fellow looks like, I'm guessing. Do tell me you at least know his name, Alicia."

Ignoring Gregory's sardonic tone, Alicia smiled sweetly and said, "I'm told he goes by the name of Dr. Beauchamp, although I think it may be safe to assume he will have changed that, since he is in hiding."

Upon hearing the name, Gregory gave out a breathless cough and began to choke on his mouthful of cake. As his face turned a peculiar shade of puce and his eyes began to bulge, fat, golden crumbs sprayed from between his lips, most of which, thankfully, were caught by the thick bush of whiskers around his mouth.

"Oh my!" Alicia exclaimed. "Are you all right, Gregory?" Jumping to her feet, she commenced thumping on his back in the hopes of dislodging the cake caught in his throat.

"That's doing him no good," Edmund's voice chipped in.

"Not now!" The words spilled from Alicia's mouth before she could check herself; she was somewhat distracted by Gregory's choking—he was grasping at his neck with clawed hands, as if making ready to rip it apart to let in much-needed air.

"Get him to his feet and stand behind him," Edmund instructed.

"*What*?!" Alicia barked as Widow Atkinson came scurrying in to see what all the kerfuffle was about; her mouth dropped open almost as wide as Gregory's at the sight that greeted her.

Alicia managed to struggle Gregory to his feet, although she feared he may collapse at any moment. Her face was a mask of absolute panic as she pounded upon her companion's back with such force that she feared his spine might crack.

"Wrap your arms around him," Edmund urged. "Grasp your hands together beneath his ribs."

"I can't do that!" Despite the circumstances, Alicia was shocked at her fiancé's suggestion of immodesty. A doctor's wife embracing a single young man in such a way? And her husband's colleague, no less!

"Unless you wish to see Gregory die, you must do as I say, Alicia." In direct contrast to her panicked state, Edmund's voice was smooth and calm, which helped her to focus. "His life is in your hands . . . *literally.*"

All too conscious of the elderly widow looking on, Alicia curled her arms around Gregory and clasped her hands beneath his weirdly heaving chest. Gregory's body felt heavy and taut against her, as if the poor chap were truly in his final death throes.

"Now squeeze!" Edmund said.

Alicia squeezed.

Nothing.

"Imagine you are attempting to crush him in two, Alicia!"

As Alicia heaved with all her might, her thumb knuckles digging deep into Gregory's diaphragm, his chest let out an almighty, wheezing cough, and a sodden lump of honey cake flew from his mouth with astonishing velocity.

"Well done, Alicia!" Edmund's praise echoed in Alicia's ears to compete with the near-deafening sound of her thumping heartbeat.

Gasping for breath like a drowning man, Gregory collapsed back into his chair and his face quickly regained its more natural colour. "Thank you . . ." he managed to wheeze out between coughs.

"Take a sip or two of this," Alicia pressed the cup of chocolate into Gregory's hand, which he gratefully took and then slurped down three large mouthfuls to calm his aching throat.

Trembling ever so slightly, Alicia sat herself back down opposite her husband's friend, who she thought looked incredibly relieved to be breathing once again. "Do I take it from your reaction you know Dr. Beauchamp?" Gregory had stopped coughing, yet still clung to the cup of chocolate as if his life depended upon it. "Or do you make a habit of choking on cake at breakfast?"

Gregory gave her a weak smile. "I know *of* the doctor," he told her, his voice hoarse and rasping. "He was one of King George's physicians up until quite recently. Our paths crossed on occasion, but I never really got to know him at all."

"What happened to him?"

Gregory shrugged. "One day he just wasn't there. No one at the palace said a dicky bird—it was like he'd never existed at all."

"And you don't find that strange at all?" Alicia felt a little bad for grilling him so soon after his brush with death, but she was all too aware of time running out, and what was at stake.

"Not in the least, Alicia. It happens all the time in palace circles," Gregory explained. "Physicians come and physicians go on an almost monthly basis—pretty much the only constant is our lunatic king. Beauchamp was simply one of dozens who have flitted through the king's chambers since the madness took hold of his poor old brain—with every new doctor comes the promise of a cure, yet so far, not one has managed to make good on that promise."

Naturally, the machinations of the crown's inner circle were as alien to Alicia as the northern city in which she found herself. Sworn to secrecy by royal contract, as well as the Hippocratic Oath, Hilary had spoken very little of what went on within Buckingham Palace. This was especially true in respect to the king himself. Suffice it to say, Alicia found Gregory's explanation perplexing.

"May I be so bold as to ask you something?" Gregory fixed Alicia with a quizzical gaze.

Worried a little, Alicia was in no mood to defend her decision to travel all the way to York on what Gregory might think to be little more than a wild goose chase, nor did she intend to reveal Edmund as the source of her information. "Of course, you may," she replied.

"What was that you did to save me from choking?" Gregory asked. "How did you know to jolt the diaphragm in such a way as to cause it to spasm like that?"

"Truly, I was not thinking, Gregory," Alicia fibbed. "I acted purely upon instinct—perhaps it was knowledge I gleaned from listening to Hilary."

"I am a doctor as well as your husband," Gregory steepled his fingers below his nose, "and I know nothing of such a procedure to prevent choking."

"Then I have no clue at all, my dear Gregory—but you can be grateful I did it at all, otherwise I rather fear we would not be having this conversation." Alicia said a mental thank you to Edmund, who was silent once more. She took a mouthful of honey cake—far smaller than Gregory had attempted—and sipped at her chocolate while Widow Atkinson disappeared back into her kitchen.

"Also, whilst you were saving my sorry hide from death's door . . ." Gregory's eyes were still very much upon Alicia's, "who on earth were you talking to?"

Chapter Seventeen

Alicia's third surprise of the day was the discovery that it was no colder in the north of England than it was in the south. Upon stepping out onto uneven cobbles of The Shambles, she found the January weather to be just as unpleasantly inclement as any she'd endured in and around London. The sky was a dark, foreboding grey filled with swollen clouds that threatened to dump what could easily be sleet or snow onto the city below. The wind that whipped through the narrow streets of York was bitter and cruel and pinched at the nose like icy fingers.

She had deftly dodged Gregory's question by declaring breakfast to be over and getting to her feet. She'd placated him by saying she had spoken out in her blind panic at seeing him in such distress so she would not swoon—in short, she had spoken to only herself. Playing the weak little woman card seemed to alleviate her companion's inquisitiveness, and no more was said of the incident after that.

Alicia's secret was safe—at least for the time being.

"So . . ." Gregory said as he blew into his cupped hands to warm them.

"So?" Alicia furrowed her brow.

"Where do we even start looking for Beauchamp, or whatever he may be calling himself?"

It was a very good question indeed. How *does* one go about locating a fellow who simply didn't want to be found? Dr. Beauchamp had travelled two hundred miles away from home and everything he knew to escape . . .

Escape what, exactly?

Alicia had an inkling that if she knew that particular nugget of information, they would have a far better likelihood of tracking the gentleman down.

"There's a haberdashery on a small side street over by the minster," Edmund told her.

Of course, she couldn't reply. Alicia wasn't sure if Edmund could read her mind or not so she had no way of communicating with him without having Gregory thinking she was conversing with herself again and quite mad.

"Just *listen*," Edmund's voice soothed. "I'm not going to get offended by you not responding to me. We can't dilly-dally around niceties if we are to save Hilary. I'm sure you'll agree."

Alicia risked a nod whilst Gregory was distracted by the mouth-watering array of pork pies neatly arranged in the window of the pastry shop adjacent to Widow Atkinson's guesthouse.

"Then we are in agreement," Edmund told her. "Now, the haberdasher's is somewhere along Deangate. The proprietor has had dealings with the doctor since his arrival in York, and so that ought to be a good place for you to start."

"This way," Alicia announced, startling Gregory from his pie-induced trance. "We head toward the cathedral." She wished Edmund's views of the future could be a tad less vague—it would save her a lot of time and effort following cryptic clues and she could hurry back to London before . . .

She stopped herself short of thinking *before it was too late*. She couldn't afford to think that way, certainly not now that she was doing something positive.

"Are you sure?" Gregory asked her.

"Absolutely," Alicia said with conviction and strode off in the general direction of York Minster, which was hard to miss because its imposing outline dominated the city's skyline just as it had for almost six hundred years.

"I can't believe it took almost two and a half centuries to build a church," Gregory said as they walked apace along Stonegate. The cathedral took up all their view ahead, its huge stone spires poking up into the grim sky as if admonishing the clouds for spoiling the day.

"It's a little more than a church," Alicia laughed. "Just look at the size of the place!"

She was correct, of course. York Minster was far more than just a church and was a more than fair comparison to St. Paul's Cathedral and Westminster Abbey back home in the capital. Constructed of pale stone and adorned with spiked turrets, ornate arches, and the most spectacular stained glass Alicia had ever seen, the minster was the perfect example of gothic architecture. She wished they had time to spare to venture inside to explore and maybe say a prayer or two for Hilary. The building was so magnificent that she could imagine God might make it His preferred northern residence.

"A haberdasher?" Gregory stood outside the small shop with a narrow door that was situated in the centre of a row of houses on Deangate. At the end of the terrace nearest the minster sat the Dean of York's residence, which was in itself a superb building.

"A haberdasher," Alicia repeated jokingly.

"Are you quite sure?"

"As sure as I can be." Alicia gave the door a gentle push and, as it swung open, there came the soft, tinkling chime of a little brass bell situated above its frame.

"Can I help you?" A timid voice drifted out from amongst the clutter of rolls of felt, silks and cotton, ribbons and fancy bows, threads of countless colours, and every conceivable type of button it was possible to hold under one low roof. Alicia imagined the place might well have existed upon that very spot unchanged over the centuries—and most likely run by the current proprietor's forebears—long before the plans for the minster had even been drawn up. It carried within its cramped, lumpy walls the wonderful smell of its history, along with the dry scent of dust that could tell so many fantastic tales, if only dust could talk.

"We are looking for someone," Alicia told the skinny old man who materialised from between stacks of gaudy silks piled all the way to the ceiling; it was as if the cloth itself was holding up the building.

"You might wish to be more specific, young lady," the haberdasher said with nary a hint of humour. "There are many people in York—that you are seeking just one in particular makes for an impossible task, wouldn't you say?" Eying Gregory with some suspicion, the old man stopped his approach a stride or two away from Alicia.

Alicia studied the old man's face, which she thought may have been quite kindly once. However, time had been less than generous to him, as his wrinkled features resembled something more akin to an old leather satchel than human skin. His eyes were dulled and as grey as the sky that brooded outside his establishment. His wispy white hair was sparse atop his crinkled scalp, and his stooped posture looked to be quite painful. Around the haberdasher's neck hung a long, cloth tape measure, and pressed over his left eye was one of those monocles that had been all the rage in Germany last century—the old man had to scrunch up his wrinkled old face just to keep the thing in place.

"He is a Londoner," Gregory chipped in. "An average sort of fellow of medium height and medium build—"

"I really don't think that's helping much," Alicia stopped him short. "Is there anything else you can remember about Dr. Beauchamp—anything a little more *distinctive*?"

Gregory shrugged his skinny shoulders so hard his entire body heaved. "If I remember correctly, Dr. Beauchamp has a small scar above his upper lip . . . on the right, I believe. There was a rumour amongst the palace physicians he'd acquired it in an altercation over his dalliances with a nobleman's wife—he was quite the ladies' man, Dr. Beauchamp."

"Ahh, you must mean *Mr. Crauford*," the old haberdasher said with a wry smile. "Why, he amused me with that very tale when he very first called in. I'd enquired as to his business here in York, and he advised me he was going to be staying a while."

"Did he say he was a doctor?" Gregory enquired.

"He did not, my good man," the haberdasher told him. "As a matter of fact, I seem to remember him telling me he was a factory owner of some sort, although he hardly looked the sort."

Alicia wondered just what a factory owner ought to look like. "Did he say where he was staying?" she asked.

The old man's face crumpled as he mulled over the question; all the while, he fiddled with the tape measure and the neat array of shiny pins in the lapel of his jacket. "I do not believe he did, other than to say he was ensconced in the upper rooms of a tavern within the city walls."

"And how many taverns are there in York?" Alicia's heart sank even as she asked the question—there were bound to be a great many.

"Honestly, I have no idea, young lady," the haberdasher told her. "Whilst I was one to frequent such establishments in my younger days, as you can see, those are far, far behind me now. Taverns come and go. They change hands at the turn of a card or strike of a cock's spur these days—it can be impossible to put a number to them from one day to the next."

"And you have no idea at all in which establishment Dr. Beauchamp—"

"Mr. Crauford," the haberdasher corrected her.

"Whatever name he prefers to go by—do you have anything at all to help us? Time is of the essence, you see, and it is quite imperative we locate this chap." Alicia was trying her darndest not to sound too much like an emotional, desperate woman, although she wasn't sure she'd succeeded.

"He struck me as a young man who had very little desire at all to be located," the haberdasher said. "He's most definitely a fellow with secrets to keep—after all my years in this shop, I know his type when I see them. I expect that the nobleman with whose spouse Mr. Crauford was carrying on would be, without a doubt, seeking retribution for the slight upon his wife and his family's good name and standing. Hence the young man's purchases that day."

"You think he's running from an aggrieved cuckold?" Gregory asked.

"Gregory!" Alicia was taken aback at her companion's use of such a coarse word in genteel company.

The haberdasher dismissed the supposed offense with a flap of his hand. "That is precisely my thought on the matter," he said.

"And what purchases did he make?" Alicia pressed.

"From me, it was a brand-new suit and cotton shirt, and no expense to be spared—he picked those up from me just yesterday. He had also enquired as to a reputable milliner in the city, and I referred him to my old friend Josiah Woodburn on Goodramgate. That man makes the finest hats between here and Newcastle. I can tell you, and he certainly didn't disappoint Mr. Crauford. He brought along the stovepipe hat Woodburn had made for him, and it was most splendid indeed."

"Might the milliner know of the doctor's whereabouts?" Gregory was becoming quite the sleuth.

"I would highly doubt it," the haberdasher replied with an upturn of his pale, thin lips. "Poor old Woodburn has been in the business since his father took him on as an apprentice aged six. The man may be the very best, but he is also rather mad. It's an occupational hazard with many a milliner, I'm afraid. Suffice it to say, even if he did remember something of the Londoner, anything he was to tell you would have to be taken with an enormous pinch of salt." Looking around the organised chaos of his own establishment, the haberdasher added, "Which is why I'm awfully pleased my ancestors chose buttons and bows over hats."

"Oh." Alicia was crestfallen. It would be an impossible task to visit every tavern in York on the off chance of bumping into Dr. Beauchamp, or even someone who could vouch for his patronage. He was clearly determined not to be found and had taken himself to the perfect city in which to achieve that.

"Thank you for your time, Mr. . . ." Gregory said. "I'm so sorry, I have forgotten your name." He appeared more than a little embarrassed by the fact.

"I didn't give it to you," the haberdasher replied with that thin-lipped smile again. "But, then again, neither of you asked, so . . ."

"Do forgive our impoliteness," Alicia chipped in. "But this is not something we do every day."

"Is that so?" The haberdasher's eyes flicked towards the door. Alicia and Gregory had evidently worn out their welcome.

"Thank you for your time," Alicia said, head slightly bowed in defeat. Feeling as though the weight of the world was resting upon her slender shoulders, she made her way to leave the shop. She had hoped Edmund might have made some suggestion as to what she ought to have asked the old man, but he'd remained disconcertingly silent throughout her exchange—she truly wished there weren't quite so many limits to Edmund's foresight.

"Wait a minute . . ." The haberdasher's voice stopped Alicia and Gregory dead in their tracks. Gregory had just gallantly opened the door for Alicia and the tiny brass bell had signalled their impending departure like an irritating little bird. The two turned back to face the old man, who stood amidst his clutter stroking his chin, as if deep in thought.

"Yes?" Gregory urged.

"Come to think of it, there *was* something your young man said when he collected his suit."

With a loud, theatrical sigh, Gregory reached for his purse.

With another dramatic wave of the hand, the haberdasher said, "That will not be necessary, young man. Do I look as if I need your money?"

Had Alicia replied with the truth, she would have told him yes, he did actually look as if he needed every farthing that he could lay his hands on. Then again, she had little concept of what such a business would charge for tailor-made suits and such.

"I distinctly remember your young doctor making enquiries as to the city's gun shops. Now, I can't actually remember if he was seeking to purchase a flintlock pistol or a sabre, but he was definitely interested in weaponry of some description."

"Did you, perchance, give the fellow any recommendations?" Alicia asked.

"Indeed, I did, young lady." The haberdasher appeared somewhat pleased with himself for having remembered. "I pointed him in the direction of Ernest Wrottesley & Sons on Coppergate. I don't know the fellow personally, as I abhor firearms in all their guises, but I do hear tell he is of an honourable disposition."

"Are all the streets here 'gate'?" Alicia enquired, pleased to feel as if she was finally getting somewhere.

"Young lady, York is a city surrounded by a wall—what else are we to call our streets?" An odd, strained sound burbled from the old man's throat. It wasn't until Alicia had vacated the shop and was back out on the cold, damp street outside that she realised it had been a giggle.

Chapter Eighteen

"I fear this could mean only one thing." Edmund broke his silence as Alicia and Gregory made their way through the bustling streets on their way across the city. She and Gregory had just traversed Church Street by the Roman bathhouse and waylaid a local to ask directions. Thankfully, they were headed in the right direction.

"Dr. Beauchamp is preparing for a duel," Edmund continued with more than a hint of panic to his tone.

Worryingly, that idea resonated with Alicia. She had heard stories of duels between gentlemen but had never witnessed one personally. "Is it possible Dr. Beauchamp is preparing for a duel?" she asked Gregory, who appeared as taken aback as she with the notion.

"Of course," Gregory slapped his forehead with the palm of his hand in the exaggerated manner of the over-acting thespians in the comedies she so enjoyed at the Haymarket Theatre back in London. "A new suit and hat, and then pistols! How could I have possibly missed that?"

Alicia shivered as much at the idea of her time to save Hilary running out as with the bitter wind that managed to find its way beneath her thick coat. "Might it be something to do with the nobleman's wife?" she ventured.

"I'd say that would be safe to assume, my dear Alicia," Gregory replied with a concerned frown. "If said nobleman has tracked Beauchamp down to demand satisfaction from him, then pistols at dawn would be very much in the young doctor's immediate future."

"Then we have even *less* time to lose." Alicia's stating of the obvious didn't make her feel much better at all. "If he is our only hope of saving Hilary, then that hope will die with him should he catch a musket ball."

"You are assuming he will lose the duel, of course," Edmund butted in. "There is always the chance he will be victorious. Simply because the nobleman is in the right, it doesn't necessarily mean he will be the better duelist."

Even though he was quite correct, Alicia found Edmund's interruption to be a tad irritating. There really was no need for him to be quite so condescending. Of course, she had considered that to be an option. All too often, in the duels she had heard about at home, it was the perpetrator of the disrespect who walked away scot-free. The unfortunate, wronged gentleman, however, was seriously injured or even killed in the name of gaining satisfaction and maintaining honour.

"I can only hope we are wrong," Gregory said as he upped his step. Coppergate was in sight. "Or, if our theory is correct, we get to Beauchamp before his opponent."

As it turned out, and much to Alicia's chagrin, Edmund's deduction had been entirely accurate.

"Why, he purchased a fine pair of 1814 Manton duelling pistols just yesterday morning!" Arthur Wrottesley confirmed Alicia's fears. "Paid a handsome price, too—he said money was absolutely no object!"

Alicia eyed the rotund young shopkeeper with some suspicion. He was rather too jolly for a man who was nothing more than a purveyor of death and death-dealing instruments. His shop—or, more accurately, his father's shop—was filled to the brim with pistols, rifles, shotguns, and swords of every conceivable type. It was as if some twisted conjurer had taken the haberdasher's shop and magically turned all of the buttons, bows, thread, and cloth into weaponry. Arthur had announced, without either Alicia or Gregory even enquiring, that he was the youngest of Ernest Wrottesley's three sons and remained an eligible bachelor-about-town.

Ignoring the shopkeeper's obvious flirtations, Alicia had wasted no time in quizzing him about the whereabouts of the young doctor he knew as Mr. Crauford.

"I can't say I rightly know." Arthur appeared as perplexed as the haberdasher had been upon being questioned by a pretty young lady. "What business do you have with Mr. Crauford, may I ask?"

It crossed Alicia's mind to tell the impudent chap no, he may not ask. But, since he potentially had information that might well assist her in narrowing down which tavern Beauchamp was resting his head of an evening, she determined the best course of action would be to humour him. And so, she gave the young gunsmith the background to her predicament as quickly and succinctly as possible.

"Well, ain't that a rum old do?" Arthur blustered. It was as if the king's guards had arrested him personally, instead of Alicia's husband. "And you reckon this rascal, Crauford can help you?"

"I'm certainly hoping so." Playing the hopeless, fraught little woman, Alicia did everything but wring her hands in anguish, although she would have stooped to that had she thought it necessary.

Thankfully, handwringing of any sort on Alicia's part was wholly unnecessary, as Arthur seemed more than willing to help out in any way he could. He had even gone so far as to tell her and Gregory he'd gladly close the shop and join them on their quest to find Alexander Beauchamp.

After thanking him pleasantly and letting him know that would not be necessary, Alicia gave the sweet young man another prompt. "So, you *do* know where Mr. Crauford is staying?"

Arthur nodded. "Well, young miss . . . I do and I don't." If he'd not intended to by cryptic and infuriating, Arthur had failed miserably.

Since Wrottesley appeared to have taken a shine to her, Gregory had remained quiet and allowed Alicia to do the talking. Now his impatience boiled to the surface as he exclaimed loudly, "Well do you, or *don't* you?"

Arthur looked embarrassed. "Well, what I do know is he's staying in rooms above a tavern somewhere on the banks of the river."

"The Ouse?" Gregory asked.

"That's the only river I know of," Arthur replied with a silly, lop-sided grin. "I recall he was worried the water was looking high and that darned river bursts its banks every year—oops, sorry, miss." Averting his eyes from Alicia in shame at his uncouth language, Arthur pretended to find something to do behind the counter with an untidy heap of receipts.

"There must be a great many taverns on the riverbank," Alicia urged. "Is it at all possible you caught which one Mr. Crauford has chosen?"

Arthur thought for a moment, and then said, "I'm sorry. To tell you the truth, I don't believe he did actually tell me. Not that he was being particularly evasive—the subject just didn't come up."

Again, Alicia sighed out her frustration. Edmund was being no help, and she knew in her heart there must be dozens of taverns on both sides of the Ouse. If Beauchamp was facing a duel sometime soon, she and Gregory simply wouldn't have time to reconnoitre each and every one.

"He did say he had to have a stable, though," Arthur offered. "For his horse . . ."

"Naturally." Sometimes, Gregory Sedgewick just couldn't help himself. Alicia gave him a gentle nudge in the ribs with her elbow.

"Sounded to me as if he was planning his getaway," Arthur postulated. "Although, why would he buy the pistols if he doesn't intend to face up to his responsibilities?"

"Perhaps he aims to win," Alicia said. "And then to race back to London, having discharged his duty to the aggrieved party?"

"Happen so." Arthur seemed satisfied with that scenario and returned his attention to the receipts. "Are you two good folks going to buy something?" he asked.

"I'm sorry, no." Alicia felt she ought to purchase something from the fellow, seeing as he had been such a big help. However, there was nothing at all amongst the veritable cornucopia of death-dealers she could even begin to imagine possessing.

Gregory pulled out his purse and fished out a few coins. "I'll take this fine dagger, if I may." He pointed to a rather vicious, curved dagger with an ornately carved, stag horn handle. It sat resplendent atop its leather sheath on the counter.

"Gregory?" Alicia was shocked.

"It is only right and proper we purchase something from Mr. Wrottesley—he has been incredibly helpful and allowed us to take up his valuable time." So saying, Gregory placed the coins upon the well-worn, wooden counter and picked up the knife.

"A wise choice, sir," Arthur said as he took Gregory's money. "Especially if you intend to visit the riverside taverns this evening. All sorts of undesirables, thieves, and rogues frequent those establishments."

"I sincerely hope it will not be needed." Gregory slid the dagger into the sheath and secreted it within his coat. "Thank you for your time, young man, and we bid you a good day."

"It's been my pleasure." Arthur looked straight past Gregory to smile fondly at Alicia. "Do call in again sometime soon."

"Thank you, Arthur," Alicia replied by means of a noncommittal farewell. She had absolutely no intention of ever setting foot in such a dreadful place again!

Chapter Nineteen

As things transpired, there were only four taverns with stables on one side of the Ouse, and five on the opposite bank. And, with luck finally on their side, Alicia and Gregory managed to hit upon just the correct one after only three likely drinking establishments. Gregory had insisted upon partaking of a flagon of ale at each and was well on his way to becoming quite tipsy.

The tavern, situated a mere handful of strides from the river, was on Coney Street, not too far from Low Ousegate. It was rather grandly named The Peacock and sported a faded old sign above its door, which depicted the magnificent bird in all its colourful glory. Alicia assumed the tavern had once been somewhat more wholesome than the den of iniquity it had become, and its name had *not* been chosen ironically. Still, as unpleasant as the dim, dank, beer-smelling place was, she had to be grateful for it being the one at which the elusive Dr. Beauchamp/Mr. Crauford had decided to rest his weary head upon fleeing from London.

"Aye, he's a well-to-do bloke all right," one of The Peacock's patrons—who had introduced himself as "just Mick"—told Alicia and Gregory. They had enquired about anyone from London who may be staying in the rooms above the tavern, or even who had taken to drinking there of an evening.

"And he said he was a doctor?" Gregory pressed the drunkard.

"Now, I didn't say that," Mick replied with a cackle. "But if you was to see your way towards buying a poor old man a drink, then I may just remember some of the particulars."

With a heavy sigh, Gregory waved over the grotesquely overweight landlord and instructed him to pour another pair of ales. "Are you sure you don't want a drink, Alicia?" Gregory asked.

Alicia eyed her companion with distaste. She felt terribly out of place in the tavern, since such questionable establishments were not frequented by young ladies of her social standing. Alicia knew her poor mother and father would throw an absolute fit if they ever found out she'd been in any of York's taverns. It was not how they'd brought her up, and with her being a doctor's wife, too!

"I'm perfectly fine, Gregory, thank you. I'd rather we find out what we need to know and be on our way, if that's all the same to you," Alicia replied. Her eyes roamed about the tavern to see if anyone seemed out of place and could possibly have been the man they were looking for. Of course, Gregory would be able to pick Beauchamp out, unless he'd affected a disguise of sorts to evade those he was fleeing. In that case, the best she could hope for was happening upon a young man who looked like he obviously wasn't meant to be there.

"I remember him now," Mick piped up as he took a hearty swig of his fresh ale. He let out a loud, resonating belch, which brought about a raucous cheer from his fellow drinkers. "He was as posh as you, too, and spoke like some common costermonger, he did . . . *''ow's ya father, apples an' pears, strike a light!*'" Mick guffawed deafeningly at his terrible cockney impersonation, as if it was the funniest thing that had ever been uttered.

Alicia scowled at the drunken man and at Gregory who, in his own inebriation, appeared to have found Mick's crude emulation of the London accent to be highly amusing.

"I really don't think that's our man," Gregory said, his face falling with disappointment. "I didn't know the fellow all that well, but I was acquainted with him enough to know he was far more well-spoken than that. If I recall correctly, he actually came from a long line of landowners and city gentlemen."

"Ah, well here's the thing," Mick said with a conspiratorial whisper. He leaned in close to Alicia and Gregory—uncomfortably close. Alicia wrinkled her nose at the powerful, sour stench of the man's beer breath, which had the bile rising along her gullet and her stomach turning somersaults.

"What is?" Gregory was clearly in no mood for theatrics. The mood had turned ominous as the winter darkness swept over the streets of York at the turn of four that afternoon. It was late, both he and Alicia had experienced quite the day and the three beers he'd downed over the course of their quest were taking their toll.

"I may be a drunkard." Mick took another long, gulping drink from his flagon, as if to underline his point. "But I ain't stupid." He tapped his forehead with one long, grubby finger. "I knows a man whose trying to hide his true voice, and yon doctor—or whatever he claims to be—was putting on a pretend accent like there was no tomorrow." With another slurp of beer and hearty laugh, Mick slammed his pewter flagon down on the roughly hewn bar top and stared forlornly at its empty inside.

"Another beer for my friend." Gregory gesticulated to the landlord, who lumbered over to refill Mick's flagon. He eyed Gregory's drink with suspicion, as if anyone merely sipping at their beer was somehow inherently untrustworthy.

"It's my reckoning your friend didn't want any of us knowing what his voice sounded like, but my ears were telling me he was as high class as the other posh bloke in here last night asking after him." Mick's eyes sparkled as the landlord placed the refreshed beverage in front of him and swiped up the array of coins Gregory had laid down from the sticky bar.

"What posh bloke?" Alicia's eyes narrowed as she scrutinised Mick. It was entirely possible he was building up his part to string them along to procure more free ale.

"Well, he was much posher than either of you two—no offence—spoke with plums in his mouth as my old mum used to say, God rest her soul." Making a clumsy sign of the cross over his chest with one hand, Mick plucked his beer from the bar with the other and downed half of it in one go.

Gregory waited with growing impatience for the chap to finish drinking. "What did this fellow look like?" he asked.

Mick screwed up his face as if there was a bad taste in his mouth. "He looked *posh*. I thought I'd told you that."

"You said he *sounded* posh," Alicia butted in.

"It's the same thing."

"No, it is not." Alicia, too, was growing impatient with the drunk.

"Well, it's *implied*," Mick slurred. "I'd have thought a pair of well-heeled southerners like you would have grasped that." He let out another hearty chortle at the expense of Alicia and Gregory.

"Can you tell us *what* he looked like?" Alicia pressed.

"I already told you . . . he looked *posh*." It was Mick's turn to sound impatient. "How many more times do you want me to say it?"

Alicia harrumphed. It was somewhat apparent they were not going to get any sense out of the drunken fellow—his poor brain must have been terribly pickled from all the years of heavy drinking. Hilary had often warned her of the dangers of the demon drink, and how it ravaged the human body—often over a glass wine, which he did not consider to be anywhere near as dangerous as the ales and gin of which commoners partook.

"I'll tell you both this for nowt, though," Mick narrowed his eyes and stroked at his chin. "I didn't much care for the cut of the man's jib, I can tell you. And if he's duelling yon doctor friend, my shilling's on young Crauford being hauled away in a wooden box."

"So, he *is* duelling?" Alicia's fears were realised. She had been hoping Edmund's assumptions as to Beauchamp's intentions in York had been incorrect.

"Aye," Mick replied with a sage nod. "Tomorrow at dawn, as it happens."

"Where?" Gregory demanded.

"Do you know nowt about our fair city?" Mick, the stinking drunk on the wobbly old stool, actually looked offended.

"I'm sorry, Mr. . . . *Mick*," Alicia placated. "We only got in late last night, and we've had such a wearisome day trying to track down Dr. Beauchamp. Could you be so kind as to tell us where a duel may take place in York?"

"Clifford's Tower, of course." Mick drained the remaining dregs from his flagon and slammed it down upon the bar to attract the landlord's attention once more. "It's where all the knobs go to settle their scores. And if what I've gleaned about the upper classes over the years is right, they're all taught how to fence and shoot straight before they can even walk. Yon doctor won't stand a cat in hell's chance against such a bloke."

"Are either of them here tonight? In the rooms upstairs, perhaps?"

"Nah." Mick studied the empty flagon before him.

"Are they likely to return?" Gregory added.

"Can't speak for the posh gentleman, as he's not staying here, but Crauford, or whatever it is you're calling him, might be back sometime as his horse is in the stables out back—in case he gets cold feet and makes a run for it, I'd imagine." He chuckled to himself at that one.

"Perhaps, then, we should await his return?" Alicia hated saying those words. The last place she wished to spend the remainder of the evening was The Peacock Tavern, associating with drunkards and women of ill repute.

"I wouldn't bother if I were you." Mick must have read her mind. "He's out enjoying what's probably his last night on earth—you'll be lucky if he comes back at all before dawn."

Gregory looked at the disappointment in Alicia's eyes. "At least we know where he will be in the morning," he said.

"I suppose we do." Alicia was torn between her desire to be gone from the horrible pub and an overriding need to find out what Beauchamp could possibly know that would save her husband.

"You'll have to get there nice and early," Mick weighed in. "Before the pistols are cocked and the seconds have tried their best. Otherwise, you'll both have nowt more than a corpse to speak to."

Alicia shuddered at the very thought. To have come all that way, tracked down their quarry, only to have him die in some silly dispute would be too much for her to bear.

"Then that is what we will do," Gregory declared. "We shall return to The Shambles forthwith and request that Widow Atkinson knock us up before cockcrow. We can be at this . . . Clifford's Tower well before dawn."

Alicia felt utterly relieved at the notion. She could be away from the riverside taverns and all their unpleasant clientele, get something into her stomach, and retire for the night. “Thank you so much for everything, Mick,” Alicia said.

“My pleasure, young miss,” Mick replied with a less-than-subtle tap at his flagon with split, filthy fingernails.

“Come along, Gregory.” Alicia took hold of her companion’s elbow and guided him away from the bar before he could put his hand in his pocket one last time. They had the information they needed, and Mick the Drunkard could buy his own darn beer.

Chapter Twenty

Supper at Widow Atkinson's guesthouse was another nice, simple affair. It comprised calves' foot soup seasoned with jelly, wine, lemon, and a whole host of spices Alicia struggled to discern, although she was positive she could detect just a touch of saffron hidden in there. It all made for a welcome relief from trudging around the bitterly cold streets of York and frequenting those ghastly ale houses and riverside taverns.

Gregory had been the perfect gentleman, navigating with skill across the city in the dark to deposit them safe and sound at the guesthouse. Alicia found the closeness of the buildings along The Shambles to be dark, eerie, and quite foreboding in the night, more than she'd realised upon their arrival the previous evening. Perhaps, having discovered a little about York's grimy underbelly, she was viewing the picturesque city through more cynical eyes?

"Thank you so much for today, Gregory," Alicia said between sips of Widow Atkinson's simply delicious soup. "You have been terribly patient with me."

"And with the odd bunch of fellows we have encountered, I think you'll find." Gregory smiled across the table at Alicia and broke off a chunk of bread from the far-too-big loaf the old widow had provided as an accompaniment to their soup.

"Indeed so." Alicia returned the smile. Considering her very first impressions of Gregory, what seemed to be a thousand years ago, she was unspeakably grateful for his company on the trip upon which Edmund had insisted. There was absolutely no way on earth she could ever have traipsed around those awful taverns all by herself let alone converse with the drunkards there.

Speaking of Edmund, Alicia found herself missing his soft, soothing voice in her mind. While it made her feel a tad guilty at harbouring his secret presence whilst her husband was incarcerated, she nonetheless welcomed his guidance and had come to look forward to his appearances. Still, she told herself, it was almost ten o'clock at night, and she supposed even ghosts who dwelled in lakes had to sleep sometime.

"I have to say, I am somewhat concerned about this other fellow who is seeking Beauchamp," Gregory said. "I can only assume his intentions are quite sinister."

Alicia scraped the last drops of soup from her bowl, her spoon grating on the smooth China bottom. Had she been at home alone, she would have picked up the bowl and slurped every dreg. She knew that would have been unseemly and most unladylike in a public place—even though the only possible witnesses were Gregory and Widow Atkinson. "I'm afraid I have to agree," Alicia replied. "One can only hope we get to the doctor before he does."

"Or, before he catches a musket ball tomorrow morning." Gregory, too, finished the last of his soup. He glanced towards the kitchen with a sparkle of hope in his eyes. As if by magic, Widow Atkinson appeared through the doorway carrying her black, cast-iron soup pot.

"The odds do seem to be stacked firmly against poor Dr. Beauchamp," Alicia was forced to concede.

"And henceforth stacked against us," Gregory replied with great sadness. "If the sinister fellow has spoken with any of the same gentlemen as we have, then he, too, will know precisely where to find Beauchamp."

"Then it is imperative we get to Clifford's Tower earlier than early." Alicia considered partaking of another bowl of soup but decided against it just as the old woman was about to ladle out a fresh portion.

"I think I shall retire for the night, if that's all the same to you," Alicia said with a friendly smile and wave of her hand. "The soup was divine, though."

Widow Atkinson served Gregory and shuffled back to the kitchen with her pot. Just why she'd seen fit to lug the obviously heavy pot to the table instead of bringing out another bowl, Alicia couldn't quite fathom.

"Before you go, Alicia," Gregory said quietly. "There is something I would like to say to you."

Frowning her concern, Alicia said, "What is it, Gregory? Please don't tell me you are weary of our quest. Not when we are so close to Dr. Beauchamp."

Gregory flapped a hand as if to dismiss such absurdity. "Nothing of the sort, my dear Alicia," he reassured. "All I wished to say is that, should the very worst happen and your poor, poor, husband be hanged or shipped out to the colonies, I would consider it an honour if you would allow me to take care of you."

Alicia was taken aback. Was Gregory making some kind of proposal? It was all very sweet, but . . .

"As a colleague and good friend of Hilary, I have grown quite fond of you—in the manner befitting that of a gentleman towards a married lady, of course."

"Of course." Alicia gave the man a smile, which she hoped he wouldn't interpret as encouragement. Whilst it was undoubtedly true she had come to see Gregory as much more than the annoying, weaselly little man who had the propensity to grate upon her nerves with every word he spoke, she had not entertained a single, solitary thought of him being anything other than her husband's friend. Indeed, to be truthful, Alicia had not allowed herself to think of any other conclusion to the whole series of unfortunate events than Hilary's release and full pardon. She knew in her heart that should the worst ever happen, she would never even consider marrying again.

She would have lost two loves in her life, and Alicia felt that was more than enough for anyone to bear. If God's great plan was for her to spend her life alone, then who was she to question Him?

"So . . ." Gregory contemplated his fresh, steaming soup as if, somehow, the answers all lay within.

"It is so very sweet of you to offer, Gregory," Alicia replied. "But, for the time being, all I can think of is my husband and doing everything within my power to free him from the Tower. I do hope you can understand."

"I do," Gregory said with a wan smile. There were breadcrumbs and droplets of soup nestled within the thicket of his beard. "Just know I will be here for you, and would make you my wife without hesitation if—"

"Shush," Alicia pressed a finger to her lips. "Let us not end this fruitful day with negative thoughts. I wish to fall asleep to dreams of embracing my darling Hilary once again, and of us enjoying a long and happy life together."

Gregory scooped up a spoonful of soup and held it to his mouth. "There is nothing I would love more than to bear witness to that, dear, dear Alicia," he said. "I do hope you sleep well—I shall retire myself once I have finished supper." He sucked up the soup noiselessly between pursed lips.

Getting to her feet, Alicia wished Gregory a good night and headed up the narrow, oak staircase to her bedchamber.

Chapter Twenty-One

As the icy, winter night smothered the city with darkness, the grim spectre of death stalked York's narrow, cobbled streets.

Thomas Reginald Cooper, proprietor of the oldest haberdasher in York, was awakened by an insistent knocking on the front door of the shop. He'd lived alone since his wife had departed to be with God almost a decade before and his three sons had set off to make their own way in the world. It had come with great sadness for Thomas to learn not one of his sons wished to continue the family business—it looked as if the little Deangate shop that had long been in the Cooper family would die with him.

"I'm coming, I'm coming! For criven's sake, give me a minute!" Thomas cupped a hand around his candle to prevent it from blowing out as he descended the stairs, each wooden step painfully cold against the bare soles of his wizened old feet.

Upon reaching the door to the shop, Thomas fiddled with the large iron key in its lock and swung it open. It hadn't once occurred to him that whomever it was thumping on the door at such an ungodly hour might wish him harm. Being so close to the minster, and the Dean's home, it certainly wasn't the first time he'd been awakened in the middle of the night by someone having a spiritual crisis.

"Oh, it's you," Thomas said as a dark shape stepped in through the doorway. "I'm sure whatever it is you want can wait 'til the morning. I open at eight, don't you know?"

The figure remained silent, and Thomas felt the cold, hard pressure of the fellow's hand upon his chest, gently but forcibly guiding him backwards into the aisles of the shop.

"Now, wait a minute, my good man." Thomas felt the icy prickle of fear crawl up his spine to nestle at the back of his skull. "If it's money you're after, then I have none at all down here."

For a thin chap, the intruder was strong. With a hearty shove, he sent Thomas reeling backwards between the stacked rolls of cloth, arms pinwheeling to maintain balance and prevent himself tumbling to the floor.

"What the dickens!" Thomas exclaimed. It occurred to him to shout out for help, but who would be out and about on Deangate at such an hour? All the drunks and floosies would be cavorting in the drinking establishments along the river, which might as well have been a hundred miles away for all the good it would have served the poor haberdasher. Terror gripped the old man as the trespasser walked steadily towards him, and Thomas wished, before venturing downstairs, he'd grabbed the rapier he kept by his bedside and had never once had cause to use.

Until then, of course.

Without uttering so much as a single word, the intruder grasped a fistful of tightly rolled blue cotton cloth and yanked hard upon it.

"Don't do that!" Thomas cried out and staggered back as the ceiling-high stack of cloth rolls teetered and wobbled in the darkness.

The intruder grabbed the middle roll of the stack on the opposite side of the aisle and pulled on that, too.

"*Noooooo*!" the old haberdasher's voice sounded hollow in the darkness and was quickly swallowed up by the noise of dozens upon dozens of rolls of cloth cascading down to fill the aisle and crush the very man who had tended them lovingly for so many decades.

Thomas Cooper died beneath the combined dead weight of so many rolls of cloth, his frail body no match for the relentless force as they piled down atop him. His bones snapped, his organs burst, and the very life was squashed from him like a beetle beneath a heavy riding boot.

The intruder, satisfied the job was done, slipped out into the night and eased the haberdasher's shop door closed behind him. It was as if he'd never been there at all.

Around the corner, on Goodramgate, Josiah Woodburn returned home after a night of imbibing beer and gin around the public houses to be found dotted along Bootham and Gillygate. He had made many friends there along the countless years and could be found most evenings drinking away the dwindling profits he made fashioning fancy hats for the upper-class folk in and around York. Josiah lived in a modest terrace house adjacent to the milliner's shop. He refused to live above it on account of the dangerous effects of the noxious chemical fumes that were an inevitability of his profession. Sadly, though, the mercury fumes he had breathed in for so many years had already addled the poor man's brain, and for the most part, he barely knew what day it was.

Staggering by the Holy Trinity church, which was dwarfed in the daytime by the tall, imposing towers of the minster, with his modest house in sight, Josiah didn't even register the dark figure slipping through the shadows behind him.

And, between the more than plentiful amount of alcohol the man had consumed that night and the persistent fog that clouded his mind even on the best of days, Josiah Woodburn barely registered the cold steel blade that slid through the soft flesh of his throat like a hot knife through butter.

He carried on for a dozen steps or more as a torrent of blood, steaming in the cold air, cascaded from beneath his chin to turn the front of his tailcoat into a dark, wet bib.

When, eventually, the dying milliner dropped to his knees in a spreading puddle of his own lifeblood no more than a handful of steps from the sanctuary of his front door, the dark shape slunk back into the inky shadows cast by the small church and vanished into the night.

Across the city, some forty minutes or so later, the fine, upstanding business establishment of Ernest Wrottesley & Sons went up in flames. Thanks to the copious amounts of gunpowder held on the premises, the conflagration lit up Coppergate from end to end. In fact, had it not been for the valiant efforts of the occupants of the neighbouring shops and houses dousing the flames with buckets of water, that entire side of the street might well have been lost to the fire.

Unfortunately, the youngest son of the business's founder, Arthur Wrottesley, became trapped in the upstairs rooms which he called home. The heat of the fire down below had set off one of the loaded muskets he kept in the sitting room, which had blasted the poor fellow's legs from only a few feet away with a debilitating amount of lead shot. And, thus crippled by one of his own devices, poor Arthur had succumbed to the smoke and flames as the floorboards gave way following an unearthly blast of gunpowder. The young man was reduced to ashes before the fire was extinguished.

It was quite the night in the city of York, one which would be spoken about for many years to come. Although the city had its own fair share of death and misadventures, never before had so many lost their lives in such a sinister fashion within the space of one single night. The place would be abuzz the following day with stories and tall tales about the terrifying fire, the poor old hat maker with his throat slit ear-to-ear, and of the haberdasher crushed to death by his own cloth.

But there would be no stories about Mike Fletcher—he was a consummate drunkard who spent most of his days in the riverside taverns mooching free beers from anyone foolish enough to give him the time of day. Because he had no one to miss him and because his body was found bloated and floating face down in reeds by the banks of the Ouse in Selby fourteen miles away and three days later, no one said a single word.

Chapter Twenty-Two

To Alicia, it felt as if it were still the middle of the night when Widow Atkinson roused her from a deep, dark slumber in which she'd found herself standing by the bank of Sweetheart's Lake.

Edmund had been there, of course, his face looking for all the world like the reflection of the silvery white moon that hung overhead in the cloudless, star-sprinkled sky. It had been a silent rendezvous, one in which Alicia had gained comfort from simply seeing Edmund's wonderful face and basking in his presence. She had no need for his guidance and stories of the amazing things he claimed to have seen in the future—Alicia still remained highly sceptical about all of that. She did wonder just what Edmund might have to gain by lying about such absurd things as a box that transmitted moving paintings from one side of the world to the other and huge, flying contraptions that carried hundreds of people heavens only knew where.

"Cockcrow is in an hour or so," Widow Atkinson informed Alicia as she rapped her bony old knuckles upon the bedchamber door. "Your gentleman friend is already awake and awaits you downstairs."

Hearing Gregory described like that cut across Alicia's grain. It made their whole association—and the very nature of their trip to York together—sound unpleasantly illicit and grubby. She would be glad when she had garnered the information she needed and they could be back on their way to London as quickly as possible.

Fumbling about in the dark, Alicia lit the candle by her bedside by touch alone and dragged her weary body out from beneath the toasty bedsheets. The frigid air bit into her skin with all the tenacity of a rabid dog and hung on there as she dressed.

A flickering yellow light caught Alicia's attention through the thin curtains drawn across her window. Her heart skipped—just a little, but enough for it to feel improper—and she padded across the room to investigate. Then, ensuring she was suitably attired in her plain blue dress and bonnet, Alicia pulled the curtains aside. The window was sufficiently high for anyone looking not to see she wore nothing upon her feet, which would have been most shocking indeed.

The handsome butcher looked across, gave her a friendly wave, and smiled. Alicia assumed the sudden brightness from her indecently close window had alerted him to her presence; it was too much to think he may just have been standing there, staring, and waiting for her to come to the window.

Alicia waved back and gave the butcher a smile that was altogether more cordial than before—in fact, it was decidedly friendly and had Alicia's cheeks feeling red and terribly flushed.

"Remember why you are up so early, Alicia, my dear." Edmund's sudden chastisement startled Alicia back into reality with an unpleasant jolt.

"Yes, of course." She swiftly pulled the curtains back together. Alicia felt like she'd been caught out in some wicked infidelity instead of merely exchanging good morning pleasantries with the handsome butcher across the way.

And, once again, Alicia hoped and prayed Edmund couldn't read her mind.

Upon making her way downstairs, Alicia did, indeed, discover Gregory waiting patiently for her by the front door of the guesthouse. Even at that early hour, Widow Atkinson had somehow managed to procure for them a curricle. This was an open carriage with just two wheels, pulled by a pair of fine fillies, which made the vehicle fast and agile. Although it would spirit them across the city quickly, it would be a terribly cold commute.

Gregory took the reins like a professional carriage driver and used his admirable skills to ensure they had fast passage through York toward Clifford's Tower.

Alicia pulled her coat about her shivering body as tightly as she could manage as the cold wind whipped about her and bit cruelly into her fingers and nose. As they sped through the streets, she recognised some of them from the day before. Alicia was hit by the unmistakable stink of fresh smoke and the sour aroma of brimstone that reminded her very much of the few times Father had taken her and Oliver hunting. The sickly, cloying reek of sulphur always put Alicia in mind of the sermons she'd sat through in church as a small child, as she had often imagined that was what Hell would smell like.

Looking around in the darkness, Alicia made out the faint clouds of white smoke hanging over one of the streets. It looked to her like innumerable malevolent ghosts swirling over the chimney tops and making ready to swoop down to pluck up the souls of unsuspecting citizens below.

"This looks to be the place!" Gregory sounded quite pleased with himself at having navigated the small carriage through the unknown city, to deliver them to their destination in what had seemed like no time at all.

Clifford's Tower stood atop a high, grassy mound on the edge of the city. Even in the darkness of that early morning, it looked ominous and evil like some round, white stone portent of death looming menacingly in the early morning fog.

"I supposed it had to be here." Alicia shivered as she studied the tower. It was illuminated by a dozen or so flickering lanterns around the front entrance. From within came the eerie glow of what she assumed to be yet more lanterns—it would appear the combatants were already ensconced within the roofless courtyard beyond those commanding walls.

Gregory brought the curricle to a halt, tied up the horses, and offered a gallant hand to Alicia to help her down from her seat. His fingers were as cold as hers, if not more so.

Alicia set off up the stone staircase that led up the hillock to the tower's entrance. She was keen to get to Beauchamp before the shooting began—if the drunkard's assumption about the other posh fellow was to be proven correct, this was likely to be the only opportunity she got to speak with the young doctor.

Arriving at the top of the seemingly endless steps with breath pluming from their mouths like wispy pipe smoke, Alicia and Gregory paused for a moment or two.

"Are you sure about this, Alicia?" Gregory asked.

"It's what we came all this way for, Gregory." Alicia was surprised at the question. Why in God's name *wouldn't* she be sure about it? After all, it was not she who was about to participate in some silly duel that may well result in her premature demise. "We really don't have time for procrastination—it will be dawn all too soon." And, so saying, Alicia marched into the crumbling old castle with determination set in her clenched jaw.

There were four people standing just off centre of Clifford's Tower's brown-slab courtyard, one of whom looked surprisingly familiar.

"Why, I do believe that's Sir James," Alicia exclaimed.

"Who?" Gregory wasn't keeping up at all.

"From the stagecoach," Alicia reminded him. "He rode all the way from London with us, and you don't recognise him?"

Gregory made a big show of screwing up his eyes to scrutinise the tall fellow in the top hat and dandy tailcoat who stood side-on to them. Sure, the light from the lanterns was not the best, but it was unmistakably the enigmatic Sir James. Even though they'd shared a carriage with the chap for three days, he hadn't disclosed his full name. "I do declare it is the very one and same," Gregory agreed. "What are the odds?"

"That he came all this way looking for the same person as us? I'd say, given recent events, it was a particularly safe bet, Gregory." Alicia couldn't help but smile at the astounding coincidence of it all. Dr. Beauchamp truly was a remarkable young man.

"So . . ." Alicia made no attempt to keep her voice down. If any of the four chaps in the courtyard had noticed their uninvited guests, not one of them acknowledged the fact. "Which one is your doctor friend?"

"The foppish young fellow in the stovepipe hat and new suit, of course. Although, he does appear to have grown quite plump since I last saw him at the palace—clearly northern life suits him," Gregory replied. "And he is no friend of mine—merely an acquaintance."

Alicia set off across the courtyard with purpose. "Dr. Beauchamp!" Her voice echoed about the ancient, disintegrating walls and rose high up into the dark. "Dr. *Alexander* Beauchamp!"

Four heads turned in Alicia's direction, and in the dim, flickering light, she saw the glimmer of recognition in the eyes of the gentleman she knew as Sir James.

"Well, look who it is!" Sir James declared with surprise. "If it isn't young Mrs. St. John!"

"You have me at an advantage, Sir James," Alicia said as she neared the four men.

"Sir James Huntingdon-Smythe," the posh fellow introduced himself most formally. He took hold of Alicia's hand and gently brought it to his lips in greeting. "At your service."

"And what business do you have with me?" Dr. Beauchamp enquired rudely. "Can you not see I am busy?"

"Good morning, Alexander." Gregory emerged from the gloom to greet his erstwhile colleague. "It has been a long time."

The young doctor seemed surprised to see Gregory. He cast a nervous glance at the chap standing by his side. The man held an exquisitely polished walnut box in both hands, as one might a precious heirloom. The man, of middle age and wearing a shabby grey suit that had seen better days, was Dr. Beauchamp's second—which was to say he was there to mediate with Sir James's second on behalf of the two duelers. Should verbal restitution not be achieved, then both seconds were there to ensure fair play and the following of the appropriate rules.

"What brings you all the way to York, Dr. Sedgewick?" Dr. Beauchamp asked.

"You do," Alicia answered for her companion.

"Whatever business it is you have with this rapscallion, I suggest you make it quick," Sir James interjected. "For he is likely to be making his peace with the Good Lord before the sun is fully over the horizon."

"My husband is Hilary St. John." Aware she was speaking quickly to beat the imminent dawn, Alicia hoped she wasn't presenting herself as some babbling nincompoop. "He has been arrested by the king's guard and is presently being held in the Tower of London pending trial for treason."

Dr. Beauchamp seemed shocked at the news. "That is impossible!" he proclaimed, "Dr. St. John is by far the most loyal and honest fellow there possibly could be. Surely there has been a mistake?"

"That is my hope, Dr. Beauchamp." Alicia looked into the man's eyes in the anticipation of finding compassion there. "*You* are my hope. I was advised to seek you out and find out what you know that can help my husband."

Dr. Beauchamp pursed his lips in contemplation. "*Who* exactly advised you, Mrs. St. John?"

"That I cannot say, Dr. Beauchamp, and it is entirely irrelevant." Alicia's voice quavered a tad as she fought to contain her emotions. "What *is* important is anything you can tell me that will get my Hilary exonerated."

"The sun is rising, my dear fellow," Sir James said in a loud voice that Alicia thought would not be out of place in any of the London theatres.

"Please, Sir James, allow me a little more time." Alicia lowered her eyes as a sign of submission, in effect throwing herself upon the nobleman's mercy.

"Very well, but do keep it brief," Sir James grunted. "I have business to attend to in Tadcaster before lunch."

"Your husband and I had finally discovered what ails King George," Dr. Beauchamp explained. "It is nothing more than a disorder of the blood brought about by the excessive use of arsenic—you know how the king cherishes his pale appearance."

"And you can cure him?" Alicia asked.

Dr. Beauchamp nodded. "And that's what led to my undoing."

"Your undoing came about when you spent time alone with Lady Huntingdon-Smythe!" Sir James erupted, his face growing quite red.

"For which you will get your satisfaction momentarily, Sir James." Dr. Beauchamp was rather dismissive, which Alicia found to be somewhat amusing. It was as if the doctor didn't fear death at all, or he was confident he would be able to outduel his angry opponent.

Brushing aside the interruption, he continued, "My *actual* undoing was in discovering the cure for the king, and, most likely, it is the very same reason that has dear Hilary incarcerated. You see, there is a reprehensible plot to keep King George stark raving bonkers and the prince regent right where he is."

"But why on earth would anyone want that?" Alicia was perplexed by the very notion. "The man is a known idiot."

"Precisely," Dr. Beauchamp said with a wink. "With the idiot prince on the throne, the monarchy will continue to destabilise. This will allow the conspirators enough time to put a German family into power. Can you imagine such a travesty?!"

"I'm afraid I cannot," Alicia replied with a shiver at the ghastly thought.

"Should the king recover and take back the crown from his son, the entire plot will fail. That explains why every single one of the king's physicians who were party to my and Hilary's discovery have all mysteriously vanished and are presumed to be dead. Your husband and I, my dear Mrs. St. John, are the last two, apart from Gregory, of course—and just look at the predicaments we are in." He cocked a snide glance at Sir James, who had begun to pace up and down the courtyard, his shiny brown boots click clacking on the dew-dampened slabs.

"You must come back to London with us and testify before the magistrates," Alicia told the doctor.

"Alas, I cannot." Dr. Beauchamp did look to be genuinely sorry. "Were I to do so, the conspirators would have me arrested on the spot for the same trumped-up charges as your husband, and hung—most likely upon the same spot, I wouldn't be surprised."

"Then my Hilary will surely hang." Alicia opted for tugging at the young doctor's heartstrings.

"Not necessarily," Dr. Beauchamp offered. "I have the formula for the king's cure hidden away in my rooms above the tavern . . . if you found me here, then you will know which one. There are also my notes and letters—they explain everything, even the bits and pieces I have gleaned about the plot against the king."

"Then bring them back to London."

Dr. Beauchamp shook his head slowly. "I would die as surely as the sun rises, my dear, and then I would be of no use to anyone but the crows."

"You will be of no use to anyone after I have finished with you as it is." Sir James had evidently reached the end of his patience. He prodded the man to his left in the bottom with the toe of his boot, which served as a prompt for the man to speak to Dr. Beauchamp's second.

"Sir James Huntingdon-Smythe demands that Dr. Alexander Beauchamp apologise unreservedly for besmirching the good name of Lady Huntingdon-Smythe and that of the entire Huntingdon-Smythe family." The man's accent gave him away as some local oik Sir James had undoubtedly paid a few shillings to be there to satisfy protocol. The chap appeared relieved to have got through his pre-rehearsed mouthful without a single mistake.

Dr. Beauchamp's second looked across at the doctor, who shook his head. "Dr. Alexander Beauchamp declines the request of Sir James Huntingdon-Smythe on account of the fact it was Lady Huntingdon-Smythe who has besmirched *his* good name."

The declaration enraged Sir James still further. "*What*?!" he fumed. "Why, I'll take my satisfaction here and now!"

"Very well." Dr. Beauchamp nodded to his second and opened the box.

Alicia winced at the sight of the pair of dueling pistols nestled within the rich red velvet lining of the walnut box. They were without a doubt the very same pistols Arthur Wrottesley had told her about the day before. "Where may we find your notes and such?" she prompted.

"Come by the Peacock around lunchtime, and I'll be glad to hand them over." Alicia thought Dr. Beauchamp was sounding somewhat cocky for a man about to meet his maker. "Perhaps the three of us could have a beer or two together—for old time's sake, Dr. Sedgewick?"

As Dr. Beauchamp and Sir James selected their respective weapons, Alicia felt a hot wave of panic rising in her chest. "But what if . . .?"

Dr. Beauchamp shushed her with a cheeky wink. "Why don't you let me worry about that, Mrs. St. John?" he told her. "You might want to stand well back—I understand poor Sir James is quite the rotten shot."

"*I'll have your damned eyes, you blaggard*!" Sir James blustered as he stood back-to-back with his adversary. He seemed long beyond caring there was a lady present.

"Ten paces, then turn and fire," Sir James's second said, rather superfluously; everyone who was anyone knew the rules of pistols at dawn.

Alicia and Gregory scurried away to press themselves tight against the tower's dank, moss-covered wall.

"One, two, three . . ." the second counted off the steps each dueler took. As the commoner reached ten, Dr. Alexander Beauchamp and Sir James Huntingdon-Smythe spun around as quick as you like, took aim, and two shots rang out as one just as the bloated winter sun peeked over the horizon.

Chapter Twenty-Three

"Another tankard of York's finest ale for the victor!" Gregory declared as he plonked down a pewter mug on the sturdy, sticky-topped pub table. The three of them—two young doctors and a handsome doctor's wife—looked more than a tad out of place amongst the tavern's sparse lunchtime clientele. They had elicited more than the occasional curious glance since arriving there with the bloodied Dr. Beauchamp.

"I'd hardly call it York's finest," Alexander Beauchamp replied with a pained smile. "Why, I'd not even say this horse's urine is the finest in The Peacock, but it is definitely doing its job, thank you very much!"

Gregory's wiry face stretched into a broad grin. "I can assure you it came from the barrel and not the landlord's bourdalou, my old friend," he said. "Although, I must agree with you, it does carry a somewhat . . . *distinctive* flavour."

Alicia looked on as the two men jibed at one another. She had shunned even a single drop of the foul-smelling liquid that passed as beer in the tavern. Indeed, it did put her in mind of the contents of a long-unemptied coach pot. "I trust it will help to soothe your wound, Dr. Beauchamp," she said by means of bringing herself into the conversation. He had taken Sir James Huntingdon-Smythe's flint-lock ball to his upper arm, which had been expertly dug out and the hole patched up by one of the city's barbers—under instruction of both Dr. Beauchamp and Gregory, of course.

"Nothing will soothe me more than the memory of that pompous ass taking a tumble!" Dr. Beauchamp announced loudly as he took a long, noisy slurp of ale. "I certainly took the wind from his snobbish sails—I daresay it'll be quite some time before Sir James throws down the gauntlet again."

"He certainly wasn't the marksman he made himself out to be," Alicia said. She still felt queasy about the whole gruesome affair. She hadn't seen so much blood in her entire life!

She had been shocked to see both combatants fall to the cold, damp paving slabs of Clifford's Tower—in the dramatised duels she had seen portrayed in theatre productions, only one man would be hit, and he was *always* the evil character.

"I honestly thought the chap was a goner," Gregory said with a ghoulish grin.

"Bah," Dr. Beauchamp scoffed. "I barely winged the fellow. He was playing up for the benefit of his own pride, and nothing more."

"You did hit him squarely in the chest, Dr. Beauchamp," Alicia corrected.

"A perfect shot, was it not?" Dr. Beauchamp laughed. "It would seem the three years of army training my father insisted upon were not such a complete waste of time after all!"

Another hearty swig of ale followed by a loud, resounding belch saw Alicia wrinkle her nose in disgust at such public crassness.

"You are lucky his sternum got in the way of the lead," Gregory said. He had gone to Sir James's aid once he'd ascertained Dr. Beauchamp was barely injured and had quickly begun work to prevent the chap bleeding to death by stuffing torn strips of St. James's own bloodied shirt into the hole his colleague had made.

"I disagree," Dr. Beauchamp replied with a snort. "It was Sir James Huntingdon-Smythe who was the lucky one—what say you, Mrs. St. John?"

"Indeed, he was," Alicia told him. "But surely you must fear for your life now, having beaten the man in a duel. I would suggest his personal pride has been irreparably wounded along with his chest, and he will be seeking retribution for that."

Dr. Beauchamp shook his head. "Sir James has gained the retribution for which he travelled to York. He challenged the man who wronged him and sullied his family's good name . . ." He jabbed a finger at his own chest and the action made him wince with pain. "That he took a lead ball near his heart and lived to tell the tale will do nothing but strengthen his standing in the high-society circles in which he dwells."

"But he did not end your life, Alexander." The nuances of duels, retribution, and of being a gentleman were confusing to her. She found the entire thing all rather silly.

"Nor did I end his." Dr. Beauchamp was exhibiting great patience in explaining the finer points of the male ego to the young lady—between gulps of foul-smelling ale, of course. "Sir James and all the other Huntingdon-Smythes will consider the duel to have been a draw, and therefore, justice to have been done. The fellow was wounded, but not fatally, and he will smart for a week or two while his body heals, and that will be that. Sir James will not come looking for me again, and, what's more, he'll be one less person baying for my blood." He cast a sideways glance at Gregory. Alicia saw a glimmer of worry in his eyes, but the moment passed in a heartbeat. "If you ask my opinion, Sir James would do well to return to his Mayfair mansion and rein in that flirtatious young wife of his." The bravado was back in Dr. Beauchamp's voice. He drained his tankard, and with a dramatic smack of his lips, he thumped it down upon the table. "Why, if he was capable of keeping the young wench entertained at home, she would spend far less of her time fluttering those comely eyes of hers at the likes of me!"

"Alexander!" Gregory chastised with a polite nod towards Alicia.

Alicia gave both doctors a reassuring smile. Whilst she was wholly unaccustomed to ribald conversation of such a personal nature, she did find it far more amusing than the altogether more genteel, dull conversations to which she was subjected to in Hilary's social circles. Of course, Alicia had no personal knowledge of Lady Huntingdon-Smythe, only the mental image and opinion she'd formed of a titled young lady who chose to consort with the likes of Dr. Alexander Beauchamp.

"Now Sir James's family pride has gained satisfaction, perhaps you might reconsider returning to London with us?" There was hope in Alicia's voice. "You could personally deliver your findings about the king's sickness to the court . . . and testify for my husband."

Dr. Beauchamp lowered his eyes, as if intently studying the dented exterior of his empty tankard. "Alas and alack, my dear Mrs. St. John," the young doctor spoke slowly, deliberately, his speech somewhat ale slurred. "It is not Sir James and his family I fear, nor has it ever been—I fled London under a far greater threat than such foolish people."

Alicia sat forward in the hard, wooden chair. "But, surely—"

Her protest was silenced with a brusque wave of Dr. Beauchamp's hand—slip a lace 'kerchief between his fingers and he would have appeared quite the fop. "I have already explained to you, Mrs. St. John," he said condescendingly, "for me to return to the city would be to invite my certain demise. There are those who would see me dead sooner than even look at me, and I would recommend you exercise caution upon your return, my dear."

"Another ale to wet the old whistle, my friend?" Gregory chipped in. He got to his feet, his eyes scanning the bar for the landlord.

Dr. Beauchamp shook his head. "I fear I may have imbibed too much of the good stuff already. And it is not sitting too well on an empty stomach with the amount of blood I lost at the hands of that confounded barber—I'd swear he did more damage to me with that knife and blunted tweezers of his than Sir James's pistol!" His eyelids drooped as he spoke as if to further illustrate his point. "I shall retire to my bedchamber for some much-needed rest. We can reconvene around teatime, by which time I shall have gathered together the documentation you require to help your husband."

"If you would permit us to escort you to your rooms, we could collect it now?" Gregory shot a look towards the spiral wooden stairs in the corner of the tavern, which wound their way to the rooms above.

Dr. Beauchamp laughed as, uneasily, he struggled to his feet. He rested a hand upon Gregory's shoulder and said, "Do you honestly think I am that *foolhardy*? You are aware of the nature of the documents I have in my possession?"

"I have heard talk of their contents," Gregory replied. "Which is why I make the suggestion we take them off your hands right away."

Leaning in to whisper conspiratorially, Dr. Beauchamp told Gregory and Alicia, "I have secreted them in several places about the tavern—by means of ensuring their safety, as well as my own. I figure that enemies of the crown seeking their destruction—or mine—will not find it quite so easy to do so."

Gregory appeared disappointed by the news, a fact he did little to hide. "Then how are we to take possession of them and help Hilary?" He looked at Alicia for support.

"As I said, meet me here this evening, and I will have everything you both need," Dr. Beauchamp said as he wobbled away from the table in the direction of the stairs. "In the meantime, I suggest you two take in the sights of this wonderful city while you have the opportunity."

Alicia thanked the doctor for his recommendation, but she felt she had seen enough of York and its sights to last her a lifetime.

Chapter Twenty-Four

Upon returning to Widow Atkinson's guesthouse, Alicia decided to take a leaf out of Dr. Beauchamp's book and get some much-needed sleep. So, she took her leave of Gregory, who intended to take the doctor's advice and explore the city while the opportunity presented itself. He told Alicia he doubted very much if he would ever venture so far north again, and he wanted to at least be able to tell friends back home that he'd walked the entire circumference of York's Roman walls.

"Shall we reconvene in the dining room?" Alicia suggested.

"Somewhere around four, perhaps?" Gregory agreed. "I propose we partake of Widow Atkinson's good food before setting off to meet with Dr. Beauchamp. "Unless, of course, you would prefer to eat dinner at The Peacock Tavern?"

Alicia could think of nothing she'd like less than that. If the food at the tavern was to be anything close to the foul brew they called ale, then she very much doubted she'd be able to allow much of it to pass her lips, let alone keep it down. "That is a splendid idea, Gregory," Alicia said with a fond smile. "I look forward to fortifying myself with good Yorkshire food before we embark on our return journey tomorrow. In the meantime, I shall retire and hopefully catch up on a little sleep—it has been quite the day so far."

Gregory laughed a little at his companion's understatement. "Let us hope the remainder of our time in York is not quite so eventful," he said. Before Alicia was even halfway to the stairs, he was on his way back out onto the cold, hard cobbles of The Shambles.

Sleep, when it finally found Alicia, was fitful. Even though her bed was pleasantly comfortable, she tossed and turned. Her mind swirled with vivid images of the duel she had witnessed and the copious amounts of gentlemen's blood she had seen spilled in the name of idiotic pride. Alicia couldn't even begin to imagine two ladies shooting at one another at dawn over some fellow. Alicia vowed if she were to ever find herself in that situation, she would deal directly with her man's infidelity and not seek to apportion blame to some third party.

And that thought brought along with it dreams of her dear, sweet Hilary. Not that Alicia thought for even one moment her husband would ever think about dallying with another woman—it was her own guilt that plagued her thoughts. Since she had begun communing with Edmund again, a dark shadow had cast itself over Alicia's conscience. Although the conversations with her deceased fiancé were wholly innocent and for the best cause imaginable, Alicia couldn't help but feel she was somehow being unfaithful to Hilary—in spirit if not body.

She made a silent vow to herself to tell Hilary absolutely *everything* just as soon as the whole sorry affair was smoothed out and he was back home—wherever that turned out to be. And that conjured thoughts of their poor, burned-out home and just how she was supposed to break the news of its destruction to her husband.

Then, Alicia was back at Sweetheart's Lake with the warmth of the sun seeping through her bonnet, the glorious twinkle of its light playing upon the murky water as if in a vain attempt to cheer it up a little. Edmund was there, of course. His handsome, smiling face looked up at her through the rippling waters as she stood in the very spot where they had enjoyed so many lazy Sunday picnics together. Although Edmund had been with her throughout the quest to seek out Dr. Beauchamp, Alicia gained comfort in the familiar—of seeing her beloved Edmund once more at the lake.

"You must return to London as quickly as you can," Edmund was telling her. The smile slipped from his face as he spoke, which filled Alicia with a sickly sensation of impending dread.

"We are to set off tomorrow," Alicia told him. She thought it was something Edmund really ought to know, although she had little idea as to when he was by her side or otherwise. "The coach leaves at six."

"Could you not set off sooner?"

"We must meet with Dr. Beauchamp this evening," Alicia explained, as the dream sun began to dip towards the horizon. It was like its descent had been accelerated by God who wished to end the day quickly. "They told Gregory the night coach was full, and the morning coach was the soonest they could get us seated."

"Then please take care of yourself, my sweet Alicia," Edmund's voice filled her dream. "Those who wish to silence you are closing in—they may actually be closer than you think . . . if only I could see clearer into *that* future."

"Don't be so angry with yourself, Edmund," Alicia comforted. Edmund's voice carried the same tone he used to have whenever he did something inadvertently silly or foolish in front of her. He always thought such actions demeaned his masculinity to his beloved Alicia, whereas she'd found it infinitely endearing. "You have been so much help throughout all of . . . *this.* I really couldn't have done any of it without you."

"I am doing everything I can, Alicia," Edmund said with sadness in his voice. "If I could do it all, you know I would. I'm fighting with all my soul to watch out for you and to protect you from any harm."

"You are so sweet, Edmund." Alicia gazed into the beautiful eyes that shimmered beneath the surface of the lake. In the background, a duck quacked and a young couple so much in love giggled at some secret, intimate joke. "How I wish things had been different . . ."

"Had they been, you would not have met the wonderful Dr. Hilary St. John," Edmund replied.

"And neither would I be in this predicament." Alicia fought back the tears, which, although she was dreaming, felt painfully real.

"You must not think that way, Alicia." Edmund sounded most stern. "After . . . after what happened to me, I grew to believe everything happens for a reason—*everything* is part of God's great plan."

"And what kind of terrible plan would involve you being taken away from me?" Alicia sobbed.

"That much, I'm afraid I cannot tell you, and it is not really my place to question," Edmund replied. "What I *do* know is that God is always there for us when we need Him. He has always watched over you and has always watched over me. He loves us more than we can know, and He wants what is best for us. And He has given me this opportunity to help you in your hour of need, and I will be eternally grateful for that."

"I am grateful, too." Alicia felt the all-too familiar pang of guilt prickle the back of her mind. Despite the dire situation that she and Hilary had found themselves to be in, she was happy to have Edmund's company because of it.

She really had to speak with Hilary upon his release from the Tower of London and hope he would understand her dead fiancé's part in all of it.

Alicia awoke with that thought echoing throughout her racing mind. The light was already fading from the day, and she estimated it was most likely getting close to dinner and the time at which she and Gregory had arranged to meet with Dr. Beauchamp.

A knock upon her bedchamber door confirmed the assumption.

"Alicia?" It was Gregory's voice. "Are you awake?"

"I am now, Gregory, thank you very much," Alicia said irritably. She threw back the bedclothes and made ready to begin the rest of her eventful day.

"I am *so* sorry!" Gregory said through the thick oak of the door. "It's just that we agreed to meet for dinner . . ."

"It's all right, Gregory," Alicia reassured, "I do need to be up and about." She smiled to herself as she tied her bonnet tight beneath her chin and slid on her boots. For everything she'd initially thought about her husband's friend and colleague, she was finding him to be nicely attentive and rather sweet.

Chapter Twenty-Five

After a dinner comprising the finest pig's trotter stew Alicia had ever tasted, she and Gregory embarked upon what she sincerely hoped would be their final trek to Low Ousegate and the veritable den of iniquity that was The Peacock Tavern. Why on earth Dr. Beauchamp would have chosen such a dire establishment as his bolt-hole was beyond Alicia's comprehension. Although, it was possible he considered it to be the very last place anyone would look for one of the king's physicians.

Dusk had all but turned to a grim, cloud-filled night by the time Alicia and Gregory found themselves once again beneath the chipped, faded old sign above the tavern's door. A few yards beyond it, the River Ouse ran sluggishly, stinking of human waste, and unnervingly high—one more night's rain and it would surely burst its banks to invade the nearby taverns, shops, and dwellings with its nasty waters.

"You don't have to come in—you can stay out here while I get the documents from Alexander," Gregory offered as Alicia hesitated upon hearing the raucous, drunken laughter from within the pub. The night-time patrons were a much livelier bunch than the sedate lunchtime drinkers.

"You'd have me standing out here on the street like some common . . . *street girl*?" Alicia managed to keep a straight face, despite the mortified look that spread over Gregory's pinched face.

"Oh my, *no*!" Gregory blustered. "I didn't mean . . ."

Laughing, Alicia placed a hand upon his arm. "I am teasing you, Gregory," she told him. "Where on earth is your sense of humour?"

Gregory appeared to be relieved. "I thought I'd blotted my copybook there for a moment," he said with a weak smile. "Your wit is certainly much sharper than mine this evening, Alicia, despite our current circumstance." He eyed the tavern's door with disdain, and Alicia got the impression he was no keener to be exposed to the inebriated patrons within than she was.

"Shall we?" Alicia threaded her arm through Gregory's elbow and gently nudged him towards the door as if they were about to embark upon a mannerly stroll along a seaside promenade.

It was with some concern Alicia noted Dr. Beauchamp was not in the bar as promised, and it crossed her mind he may well have fled York as he had London to evade those who meant him harm. Although, how much further would he go? Newcastle? Edinburgh? Aberdeen, even?

"Perhaps we ought to ask the landlord?" Alicia suggested.

"Or maybe that serving wench may know of the doctor's whereabouts?" Gregory countered as his eyes fell upon the buxom, comely lass, who was busy serving beers behind the bar. She wore a grey blouson that was pulled down to expose her milky-white shoulders. "If I know Dr. Beauchamp well enough, that would be the more likely port of call."

Alicia followed Gregory's gaze to the young barmaid. She couldn't help but wonder which of life's paths had brought the girl to work in such an awful place, and just how much the landlord was paying her to be on public display in front of the drunk and disorderly. Still, the gal had a broad smile upon her face and appeared to be enjoying the attention her position afforded.

"Excuse me, miss," Gregory ventured upon approaching the bar.

"Two beers?" The barmaid gave Alicia a strange look, as if she were dying to ask her what *she* was doing in the tavern.

Gregory hesitated a second or so before replying, "No, thank you. We are looking for a Mr. Crauford. He is staying here." For emphasis, he pointed a finger towards the ceiling, just in case the barmaid was feeble of mind.

The girl rolled her eyes at Gregory and flashed a knowing smile at Alicia. "Oh, yes, Mr. Crauford is staying here, all right," she said. "He's been a very good customer to all of us."

"We were supposed to meet him tonight." Alicia had to raise her voice to be heard above the cacophony of strident laughter, and she was more than aware of the stares she garnered from the tavern's drinkers. Once again, she was the only woman in the place—other than the barmaid and her poorly fitting frilly blouse, of course.

"Well, he's not been down yet," the barmaid told Alicia and Gregory.

"We *really* do need to see him," Gregory insisted. "Could you bring him down for us?"

The barmaid scanned the room and the impatient customers lined up along the bar. "We don't run a fancy hotel here." She scowled. "Does this look like The London Grand Hotel to you?"

Alicia followed the barmaid's gaze and was forced to admit that no, The Peacock Tavern looked absolutely nothing at all like the luxurious city hotel.

"Then may we go and retrieve the good doctor?" Gregory fished a few pennies from his pocket and laid them upon the tacky bar top.

"He's a doctor, you say?" The barmaid appeared impressed—and somewhat surprised. "I suppose it wouldn't do any harm. Room five." With a shrug of her bare, slender shoulders, the barmaid scooped up the pennies, secreted them within the pocket of her apron, and then returned her attention to the horde of thirsty drunkards who demanded it.

The smell assaulted Alicia's nose from about halfway up the creaky old staircase leading up to the rooms above the bar. At first, she thought perhaps the ungodly reek was emanating from the Peacock's stables, or even the river, but the further up she got, the less likely that seemed to be.

Gregory appeared not to notice, or if he did, he chose to remain politely silent. *Maybe this was how all riverside taverns smelled*, Alicia thought to herself. The stink of poverty and desperation, of unwashed bodies and human waste.

The smell was worse at the door to room five, which filled Alicia with an overwhelming feeling of dread. She had smelled death before, when Edmund had passed away, and it very much put her in mind of that.

Hand shaking, Alicia rapped upon the door with her knuckles. "Dr. Beauchamp? It's Alicia and Gregory. Are you all right in there?"

The low, grunting voice from within took Alicia entirely by surprise. "Come in!" It sounded strained, horribly sick, almost like Edmund in his final moments by Sweetheart's Lake.

"Wait." Gregory grasped Alicia's arm as she reached for the doorknob, which she considered to be rather over-familiar of him. "I should go first—just in case . . ."

"I think I shall be perfectly fine, thank you," Alicia asserted herself and took no pleasure in seeing Gregory shrink back ever so slightly. So saying, she twisted the knob and pushed open the door to Dr. Beauchamp's room.

At first, Alicia wished she had allowed Gregory to enter the room ahead of her. The first thing that hit her was the sickening stench of human waste that had the pig's trotters dancing an uncomfortable jig in her belly, and the second was the terrible state of the poor doctor laying upon the filth-stained bed in the corner of the room.

"Oh my dear Lord!" Alicia exclaimed and dashed across to Beauchamp.

Gregory held back a little, as if afraid to approach. "Be careful, Alicia, it could be cholera!"

Of course, Alicia knew cholera all too well—enough to know this was certainly not it. The unfortunate Dr. Beauchamp was a terrible deathly grey colour, his shirt and pantaloons were soaked through with bloodied vomit and diarrhoea, and his body trembled with involuntary convulsions that had him frothing at the mouth.

"*Arsenic*," Dr. Beauchamp croaked as his body doubled up in pain and a surge of foul-smelling urine gushed out of him. "It's arsenic poisoning," he only just managed to say.

"What can we do?" Alicia gave Gregory a desperate look. "You're a doctor, confound it! You ought to know how to cure arsenic poisoning!"

Sadly, Gregory shook his head and stood over his old colleague. "I'm afraid there's nothing to be done here," he said quietly. "If only we had caught it sooner, we may have been able to do something."

"Don't say that!" Alicia snapped. "Especially not in front of him!"

"Dr. Sedgewick is quite correct in his diagnosis." Dr. Beauchamp's voice was barely a whisper. "I must have ingested a large amount of the stuff to get this sick so quickly. I'm afraid I have very little time left."

"There must be *something* we can do?" Alicia was very close to tears. She didn't want to watch another human being die before her very eyes, even if it was one she hardly knew at all.

Dr. Beauchamp reached out to hold Alicia's hand. His fingers were sticky and caked with blood and heaven only knew what bodily fluids he'd expelled in his sickness, but she fought against the urge to pull away.

"Take the documents," the doctor urged. He twisted his head to indicate a tan satchel in the far corner of the room, which sat adjacent to the rough-hewn dresser. "Everything is in there—including the formula we devised to save the king's life."

"And what about Hilary?" Alicia hated herself for asking the question, for thinking of herself whilst the unfortunate man lay dying covered in his own excrement.

"The documentation will exonerate your husband. There is everything in there to restore his reputation and have all of the charges dismissed by the magistrates." Dr. Beauchamp squeezed Alicia's hand so tightly that her finger joints popped. His body shuddered violently, and a viscous fountain of blood and bile spurted out from the back of his throat. "Give everything to the king's physicians—they will know what to do with it. They can cure the king and save the crown—you'll be a hero, Mrs. St. John."

Alicia fought the urge to empty her own stomach and wished Gregory would do more than just stand there looking useless. Then again, she knew from experience with her husband, a dispassionate countenance was all part of a doctor's armoury against the presence of death their calling encountered daily. It was something Alicia knew she would never be able to get used to.

"Take it now," Dr. Beauchamp urged. His grip on her hand was growing slacker by the second as his life ebbed quickly away. If Alicia had not been holding on to his limp fingers, his hand would have flopped back by the doctor's befouled side. "Alicia, take the papers and leave this place. Get yourself back to London as quickly as you can and . . ."

"I . . . We can't leave you like this." Alicia's protest had her on the verge of hysteria.

"There's nothing you can do for me now. Unless . . ." Dr. Beauchamp's eyes flicked to the duelling pistol that lay upon the nightstand—a trophy of the final victory of his life.

"*No*!" Alicia was appalled at the very idea.

"It *would* be the kinder thing to do." Gregory reached for the weapon. "Like putting an injured animal out of its misery." Slowly, deliberately, Gregory checked the pistol over, looking to see if it was loaded.

It was.

"Dr. Beauchamp is *not* an animal!" Alicia scolded. "If he is to die, then he deserves to do so with dignity."

A huge spasm contorted the young doctor's body, and he threw up what Alicia feared were chunks of his stomach. How terrible it must be, she mused, to bear the burden of the knowledge of precisely *how* you were dying.

Seeing the expression in Alicia's sweet eyes, Gregory lowered the pistol. "Alas, I cannot," he said. "The Hippocratic Oath prevents me from taking a life." Gregory offered the dying man a comforting smile. "What I can do is stay with you until . . ."

"Thank you." Dr. Beauchamp forced a smile in return. Gregory's offer to remain with him 'til the end seemed to sooth him a little.

Letting go of the doctor's hand, Alicia retrieved the satchel from the corner and made for the door. She exchanged a glance with Gregory, who sat himself down on the edge of the bed.

"Trust no one, Alicia," Dr. Beauchamp called across as she pulled open the door to room five and welcomed the relatively fresher air beyond. Glancing over her shoulder, Alicia fancied the doctor's eyes were upon Gregory at that moment, although she really couldn't be entirely positive.

"I promise."

"And wish Hilary the best of British luck from me," Dr. Beauchamp said as Alicia closed the door behind her and hurried towards the stairs. She found that she had little desire to witness the untimely end of yet another young man's life.

Chapter Twenty-Six

Much of the first day of travelling was done in silence. Alicia and Gregory shared the carriage back to London with an elderly spinster lady on her way to Wimbledon to stay with her sister who had taken ill with a madness that Alicia thought sounded eerily similar to that of King George. Of course, she didn't say as much to the old woman, who gave her name simply as Agnes, as she didn't feel in the right kind of mood to enter a long, convoluted conversation on the whys and wherefores of insanity with a stranger.

Gregory had been quiet from the moment they had boarded the coach in the early hours of the morning, although Alicia knew he shared her gratitude at putting York behind them. Certainly, it had been an intense few days, and he looked to be as exhausted as she felt.

Alicia was proud of Gregory for staying with Dr. Beauchamp to provide comfort in his final moments—as it transpired, the poor man hadn't lasted but a couple of hours. She couldn't even begin to imagine how much despatching the unfortunate Dr. Beauchamp would have weighed on her companion's mind had he done as the dying doctor had asked. Not only had the man been a colleague but putting him out of his misery would have gone against everything the

Hippocratic Oath Gregory had taken stood for. He was a doctor and man of irrefutable honour, after all.

And so, Alicia travelled with her own thoughts for company. They were occasionally broken up by a few pages of her book and long, lingering looks out of the window at the drab, grey skies and damp, foggy countryside that trundled by as the carriage made its way closer to London and her darling Hilary. Alicia always kept Dr. Beauchamp's leather satchel on her lap as an old dowager might cradle a small, equally ancient snappy lapdog. She chose not to peek inside—although, heaven knew how much she desired to, as she feared it would spark a conversation with Gregory she dearly wished to avoid. Gregory had shown little interest in the satchel—and its incredibly crucial contents—which puzzled Alicia somewhat.

Surely, she thought, as a doctor, as someone who had been party to the research contained within Dr. Beauchamp's satchel, Gregory would be eager to get his hands on the notes.

But no.

Gregory seemed as happy as she to merely stare out of the carriage window and watch the world go by or take lengthy naps with his hat tipped over his eyes.

The first night's stop was at a grim, entirely questionable, coaching inn in the heart of Doncaster, home of the famous St. Leger horse race. The establishment had but five rooms, and Alicia had found the food to be barely palatable. Supper appeared to be a stew of sorts. She dared not enquire as to it specific contents, although she was positive she'd seen a crow's beak bobbing about in the pot when the innkeeper had served it up.

Needless to say, Alicia filled herself up on the stale bread and water, while Gregory gorged himself on the awful stew, which he swilled down with copious amounts of the inn's warm, flat beer.

Other than that, and much to Alicia's relief, the stay over went without incident, and she surprised herself by managing a sound, dreamless, and full-night's sleep.

Their second stopover, in the altogether more pleasant town of Royston, Hertfordshire, did not go quite so smoothly.

The coaching inn—the unimaginatively named Red Lion—was agreeable enough; at least, as agreeable as such perfunctory places could be. It had edible food—succulent lamb shank and potatoes, which tasted as good as they smelled—a multitude of spacious rooms, each containing a large, comfortable bed, and *fresh* water in the pitcher upon the dresser. Alicia was delighted to discover the chamber pot in her room had been emptied from the previous guest, which made for a welcome change from the stale leavings she'd had to face back at the Doncaster inn—and she was confounded if she could recall the name of the place. Perhaps, she thought, it was so awful her mind had blocked it out completely. Or maybe it was like the dark, mysterious places in the ghost stories Father loved to tell at Christmastide, and the Doncaster inn had never really existed at all . . .

It may well have been that idea—Alicia's last waking thought—which brought about such peculiar dreams.

"It's been a while, Alicia, and so much has happened," Edmund said with a comforting smile. "I have missed you."

"And I, you, my dear Edmund." Alicia found herself once more gazing into Sweetheart's Lake at Edmund's sweet face. The weather, sunny and pleasant with fluffy white clouds against an egg-blue sky, warmed Alicia's face and ruffled her hair with its gentle breeze. Her feet were deliciously bare, her stockings discarded heaven only knew where, which made Alicia feel wanton and guilty all at the same time.

The lake, she was astonished to see, was totally clear, the water crisp and colourless all the way to its bottom. There, Alicia fancied she could make out the long, sleek shapes of myriad fish and eddies created by small, darting creatures.

"It was quite terrible to see Beauchamp go out like that," Edmund ventured.

"You were there?"

"Kind of." There, Edmund paused, as if gathering his thoughts. And then he said, "I mean, I *was* there, but I found myself quite unable to let you know, let alone attempt to communicate with you."

"I can't imagine what it did to poor Gregory." Alicia fiddled with her bonnet, which she held at her waist like some damp dishrag. "He has been so uncharacteristically introverted since we left York."

"It was good that Gregory stayed with him until the end. Dying alone is a terrible thing. I will be eternally grateful to have been able to end my days in your arms and be forever joined with Sweetheart's Lake."

Studying Edmund's face, Alicia thought she saw just a touch of regret lurking beneath the smile, a tinge of pain in those beautiful eyes. "You must get so lonely here all by yourself," she said.

"I have our time together to look forward to," Edmund replied, deftly sidestepping Alicia's roundabout question. "When I am with you, everything else simply melts away. And I venture into the future to take the occasional peek at what is to come, although I do admit, much of it scares me so."

"Like the horseless carriages?"

"Precisely," Edmund laughed. "And the long, snaking trains that seem to be able to run without steam or smoke—they are certainly a sight to behold! Why, I can imagine Richard Trevithick spinning in his grave at the very notion!"

"But he's not dead, Edmund," Alicia corrected him.

"Not *yet*, he's not." Edmund did sound rather mysterious. "But his bones will have been long mouldering in his St. Edmunds grave by the time his steam locomotion is surpassed."

"Sometimes I envy you, Edmund." Alicia took a step closer to the lake, a step closer to Edmund. "All the amazing things you get to see, all the places you can visit in an instant."

The smile slipped from Edmund's lips. "It all pales into insignificance against not being able to smell fresh flowers, feel the breeze in my hair, the grass beneath my feet. Nor is it adequate compensation for being unable to hold you, my beloved Alicia, or feel the heartache of watching you find love with another."

"But you will always be my first love, dear Edmund—if it were not for the cholera, we would be happily married now." As quickly as the words left her lips, Alicia regretted them. How could she even say such a thing with Hilary, her poor husband, languishing in the Tower? And even though this was merely a dream, and she was aware it was such, Alicia felt truly wretched.

Edmund fell silent for a while. His face faded a little beneath the rippling waters of Sweetheart's Lake. From the distance came the whinnying of a solitary horse, the urgent quacking of a mother duck rounding up her little ones, and a low, resonant rumbling sound that Alicia *felt* rather than heard.

"It is time for you to go." The suddenness of Edmund's voice startled Alicia. She glanced around as if expecting to see the source of the peculiar sound.

Nothing.

"You must wake up, Alicia," Edmund insisted. "You are in grave danger, and you have to awaken now."

"I am not ready to leave you, Edmund, not yet." Alicia took another step towards the lake, her bare toes peeping over the edge of the bank.

Edmund's face floated to the lake's surface, the very tip of his nose breaking its surface. "But you *must*, my love," he told her. "And upon your return to London, you must remember to be wary of those around you, especially now things have so drastically changed . . ."

"*What* has changed, Edmund?" Panic gripped Alicia's heart. "Has something happened to Hilary? Please tell me!"

Without replying, Edmund reared up from the water, his body running with cool, clear water, and levitating as by some unearthly witchcraft. He reached out for Alicia with long, powerful arms and took hold of her shoulders with fingers so strong she feared her bones would snap beneath their grip.

In the blink of an eye, Alicia found herself beneath Sweetheart's Lake. Its water invaded her nose and mouth as she attempted to cry out. Even her darling Edmund's arms about her body brought no comfort against the encroaching blackness.

Chapter Twenty-Seven

Alicia struggled from her deep sleep coughing and spluttering as if emerging from the cool, cloying waters of Sweetheart's Lake. Even as the dream state sloughed away from her mind, Alicia's skin felt uncomfortably moist, and there seemed to be a thin veil of wetness covering her face.

Wiping away the imaginary water with both hands, Alicia sat bolt upright in her bed and stared wide-eyed into the blackness that filled her bedchamber.

There.

Lurking in the corner was a shape, one that was decidedly human.

"*Hey*!" Alicia called out, fumbling down the side of the bed. Her groping hand touched upon something familiar. "Get out of here, you *blaggard*!"

The shape, a black shadow amongst the night that concealed it, shifted towards the bedchamber door.

Mustering every ounce of her strength, Alicia grasped the riding boot she'd located by the side of the bed and hurled it at the shape as it scurried for the door.

"*Ooof*!" The shape grunted as Alicia's boot hit home.

Before Alicia could locate her second boot, the intruder had slunk out through her door and pulled it closed with an almost silent, dull *thunk*.

Almost as quickly as Alicia's bedchamber door closed, it opened again. This time, it brought with it the yellow, dancing light of a candle and a familiar face.

"Gregory!" Alicia called out with relief. "There was someone in here!"

"Who?" Holding the candle out in front of himself like some bizarrely inadequate weapon, Gregory peered about the room for the scoundrel who had dared invade a lady's bedchamber.

"It was too dark to see," Alicia told him as she pulled up the bedsheets to her neck in order to preserve her modesty. "I have no idea who it could have been. I'm surprised you didn't trip over the fellow on your way in!"

Gregory shrugged and pulled a face, the flickering light and unflattering shadows making him appear like some grotesque, hunched gargoyle. "I didn't see a soul, Alicia." He made his way across the room to Alicia's bed, his stockinged feet making barely a sound on the hardwood floor. "Perhaps you dreamed the whole thing?"

Although Alicia shook her head no, she was already beginning to doubt her own eyes. Considering the vivid, disturbing dream from which she'd awakened, there was all probability she could have imagined the intruder. "If that was the case, then who did I throw my boot at, Gregory?"

Gregory perched his skinny derriere upon the edge of Alicia's bed, which, even given the extenuating circumstances, was most improper—she was a married woman! "The dreaming brain can conjure a whole host of imaginary things, Alicia." He spoke softly, in just the kind of the soothing voice Hilary said all doctors used when addressing a particularly sick patient. Only, she wasn't sick—unless Gregory's tone was intimating she might have some malaise of the brain.

"I know what I *saw*, Gregory." Alicia was most firm on the matter.

"You know what you *thought* you saw," Gregory insisted. "You are in a strange place, it is the dead of night, and I'll warrant you were having an odd dream of sorts?"

Alicia refused to acknowledge that one. It truly was no business of Gregory's what had been occupying her dreams. Although, a large part of Alicia knew her reticence was more to do with her own guilt at tarrying with Edmund than indignance at Gregory's attempts to explain away what she'd seen as nothing more than dream-induced hysteria.

"I think you ought to try to get more sleep, Alicia." Gregory patted the pillow. It was a strangely fatherly gesture, most unbecoming. "It's an early start in the morning, and once we arrive in London, there will be much to do—including a trip to the palace to seek our audience with King George."

"I really don't think I'll be able to sleep at all, Gregory." Alicia's eyes darted about the room, following the sallow light cast by Gregory's night candle.

"Perhaps if I stayed with you?" Gregory settled himself a little further upon Alicia's bed and smiled at her through his beard.

"Gregory, *no*!" Alicia exclaimed, as if scolding a naughty puppy. "That would *not* do at all!" She gripped the bedsheets tighter to her neck and locked her eyes upon Gregory's.

"Do forgive me, my dear." Gregory slipped off the edge of the bed and stood over Alicia. "I really did mean nothing by it, other than I wished to do the gentlemanly thing and remain with you in your moment of distress."

Alicia had a rather strong inkling that was not entirely true but decided the subject was best left. It was late, oppressively dark, and cold, and having had an intruder in her bedchamber, she was as wound as a clock spring. "Of course," she placated. "I must apologise for thinking otherwise. It really has been quite the stressful night."

"Indeed so," Gregory agreed. He walked backwards away from Alicia's bed, which gave her the illusion time was somehow running in reverse. "Maybe I ought to take care of that?" He nodded at the satchel Alicia had not allowed from her sight since Dr. Beauchamp had entrusted it to her. It was scrunched up in the corner like a crumpled, little old goblin.

"It is perfectly fine where it is, thank you, Gregory." Alicia eyed the satchel in the dim light of her companion's candle. "I shall place the chair against the door to prevent further intrusion, since the locks here do not appear to work." She pointed with her nose at the solitary chair by the dresser. "Now, if you wouldn't mind, I think I'd at least like to *try* to get some sleep."

With that, Gregory let himself out. Once more, Alicia was all alone in the darkness. She imagined Gregory had appeared somewhat deflated when he'd slipped from her room, although, whether it was because she had denied him the satchel or a night in her bedchamber, she was unable to make up her mind.

Chapter Twenty-Eight

January 29, 1820

The coach made good time along the Great North Road. It rode through the last of the turnpikes and into the outskirts of London well before dusk. The sky was the colour of tarnished steel, and the air was damp with the kind of fine drizzle that soaks all the way through even the hardiest of topcoats to leave a person cold, wet, and miserable.

But it was not the typical British winter weather that struck Alicia as they sped through Stanmore, Edgeware, and Borehamwood—no, it was the unusually quiet streets. There was barely a single soul to be seen.

"The flags are flying half-mast." It was Gregory who voiced the observation as he peered out through the window.

"Somebody important died," Agnes chipped in with her usual dour countenance as she squinted out through the window on her side of the carriage. "They always lower the flags when somebody important goes to meet their maker."

"Oh, dear Lord, no." Alicia's heart sank. "Please say it can't be. Gregory, *please* say it can't be." Panic gripped her heart once more as she felt hope drain away.

Gregory pulled down the window and stuck out his head to address the driver. "I say!" he shouted against the icy wind and fine rain. "My good man!"

"Aye, sir?" the carriage driver grunted from beneath his muffler. He twisted his head to look at Gregory, yet somehow managed to keep his eyes on the road at the same time.

"There's an extra five shillings for you if you take us directly to the palace."

"St. James's?"

"No! *Buckingham*!" Gregory snapped impatiently.

The driver shrugged. "There's a lot of palaces in London, sir," he grumbled. "It would be helpful if you'd specify which one. And it'll be eight."

"Pardon me?" Gregory's teeth were chattering so loudly Alicia could hear them from within the relative warmth of the carriage. She wondered just how coach drivers managed to do their jobs in the wintertime without freezing to death.

"Eight shillings," the driver reiterated. "If you want me to take you to Buckingham Palace. That's not my regular stop."

"Confound it, man!" Gregory allowed his short temper to get the better of him. "I'll give you *ten* if you get us there within the hour!"

With a click of his tongue and snap of the reins, the driver had his horses quicken their step, and Alicia felt the carriage accelerate.

"What if King George has passed?" Alicia asked of Gregory.

"Then that useless, fool son of his will be crowned successor to the English throne, of course," Gregory replied.

"No . . . I mean, what will happen to Hilary?"

"I don't see how the king's death will make any difference to his predicament," Gregory replied. "In fact, I dare say he may well receive a full pardon, as is often the case upon the death of a monarch. The new king likes to get off to a fresh start."

Hearing that news gladdened Alicia's heart a little, and she allowed a touch of that lost hope to creep back in. Peering out of the drizzle-soaked carriage window, she studied the London streets as they zipped by and held on tight to Dr. Beauchamp's old leather satchel as if her very life depended upon it.

Chapter Twenty-Nine

Alicia's heart sank as the coach pulled up outside Buckingham Palace. A small crowd had gathered at the gates and the curtains in every single one of the imposing building's windows were drawn. Atop the roof, the flags flew at half-mast, just the same as every other flag she had seen since entering the city.

"Mad King George is dead!" Agnes declared as the driver hopped down from his seat to open the coach doors. "He must be—it would be too much to hope the prince regent has been struck down by the cholera!"

Alicia stepped out, followed by Gregory. She eyed the commoners by the palace gate, who appeared to be doing little more than peer blankly through the iron railings. It was quite possible they had been paid by someone inside the palace to give the appearance of mourning—either that, or they were merely waiting for the nearest gin house to reopen following the tragic news of the king's passing.

"Excuse me?" Alicia accosted one of the would-be mourners, a middle-aged man with a crooked set of yellow and black teeth, which appeared to be on the verge of falling from his mouth. "Is it true that the king is dead?"

"Aye, missus," the man said with a roll of the eyes. "And about time, too, if you ask me."

"Well, that's no way to show your respect to our head of state," Alicia couldn't help but chastise. She had been brought up to revere the crown, no matter whose head it sat upon, and no matter how insane they were thought to be. Her father had been a devout Royalist his entire life, although that devotion had been severely tested when King George had taken ill and his son filled the newspapers with his foolhardy, inherently costly escapades.

"He was blind, deaf, and mad as a hatter," the man replied with a grin that showed off his rotten teeth to perfection. "You tell me what kind of life that is for any man, let alone the King of England, if you'll pardon me being so blunt."

Alicia was forced to agree with the little man, although she couldn't bear to think what sorry state the country was going to get itself into with the king's son at the helm. And she also worried about what all of it meant for Hilary. With the king dead and well beyond curing, what good would Dr. Beauchamp's research and magic medicinal formula do for her husband? Swallowing hard, Alicia forced herself to think more positively than that. All the while, she fought the gnawing, sinking feeling that settled in the pit of her belly with absolutely no intention whatsoever of leaving.

With little point in attempting entry to the palace, and their carriage having left them and their luggage by the gates, Alicia and Gregory had no other option than to hail a Hackney carriage apiece and go their separate ways. She had plans to return to her parents' home in Bethnal Green, whilst Gregory was to return to his digs in Whitechapel.

"Oughtn't I take care of these now?" Gregory reached for the satchel as his carriage rolled up.

"It's okay, Gregory," Alicia replied with a polite smile and just the slightest turn of her body. "I think I shall take a look through them once I get home." It struck her again that *home* no longer existed, and she was already considering her parents' house as such.

"They'll be all medical jargon and the like," Gregory pressed. "Written by physicians for the understanding of the profession alone.

Why, I would hate for you to become confused by the whole thing, my dear Alicia."

Once more, he reached for the satchel. Alicia twisted around again—more noticeably so than before—to make her intentions perfectly clear. "You seem to forget I am a doctor's wife, dear Gregory." She maintained her pleasant smile, although she feared it might start to slip the more Gregory persisted. The idea that he considered her some feebleminded little woman incapable of comprehending a few medical words was rather insulting. "I shall read through them this very evening in preparation for my husband's trial. There will be something within that shall prove his innocence."

"You are making the assumption there is to be a trial," Gregory said with a coldness to his tone Alicia found a tad disturbing. "With the king dead, it may take months—*years* even—before it ever comes before the court, if at all. And all the while, poor Hilary will languish within the Tower's walls—unless they decide to execute him, of course."

Alicia shivered—more at Gregory's harsh words than the biting January chill. "I cannot—*will* not—allow myself to think of such an outcome," she protested. "I shall make enquiries first thing in the morning as to the date of my husband's trial, and we shall be prepared to defend him. My father knows of a few good fellow barristers who will be only too pleased to defend an innocent man—even against the crown."

"Then I wish you well, my dear, sweet Alicia." Gregory took a step back to signify he knew he was beaten. "Should you have any questions as to the contents of Dr. Beauchamp's notes and research, please do not be afraid to ask."

"Rest assured, I shall do just that," Alicia said as she watched her husband's friend clamber into his awaiting carriage. "I will let you know what I find out about Hilary's trial date, too."

Gregory simply nodded and slammed the door behind him. Just as the Hackney carriage set off, Alicia's arrived behind it.

As it transpired, Hilary St. John's trial was to come around far quicker than Alicia, and especially Gregory, had anticipated.

Chapter Thirty

It was to be just two short days following Alicia's return to London.

On the positive side—and Alicia tried so very hard to remain positive—she would get to see her beloved husband, albeit in prison garb and shackles. But on the negative side, Hilary's fate would be decided upon the whim of a judge and jury mourning the death of their monarch.

"I wish I could be the one defending Hilary," Dudley Bartlett said to his daughter with sincere regret. "But it would be deemed most unprofessional were I to do so, what with him being my son-in-law and all."

"I understand, Father." As Alicia gave his hand a reassuring squeeze, her voice echoed slightly about the expansive vestibule of the Old Bailey court building. "And I have every confidence in Mr. Collings, since he comes with your heartfelt recommendation."

"Best barrister in London," Dudley declared as the elderly Josiah Collings approached from the court's doorway. He held in one gnarled hand the satchel Alicia had guarded with her very life all the way from York. Dudley peered at the old man over his spectacles. "Other than yours truly, of course."

Alicia returned her father's smile and loved him for doing his level best to cheer her up under such dire circumstances. "I am positive Mr. Collings will do just splendid," she said.

"I'm sure it will all be little more than a formality," Gregory chipped in. He had been there waiting for Alicia and Dudley before the court's main doors had even been unlocked that morning. "Once the jury sees what's contained within Beauchamp's notes, they will have no other option but to find Hilary not guilty." He offered Alicia a smile of his own, partially hidden within the thicket of that magnificent beard of his, which appeared to have been especially trimmed for the occasion.

Alicia said a cursory hello to Mr. Collings the moment he got to them. With the trial imminent, there was little time for niceties.

"I spent most of yesterday going through the papers your father gave me," the old barrister lifted the satchel a little for emphasis. Dudley had deposited the documents with the barrister upon commissioning him to defend Hilary. "I must say, a great deal of it is quite impenetrable—too much bloody medical gobbledegook if you ask me."

"But you did find something in there to exonerate my husband?" That old, familiar panic crept through Alicia once more.

Nodding, the old barrister snorted and stroked at his tidy, white beard. "It certainly shows he and his colleagues meant the king no real harm," he said. "Are you sure you can't muster any of them to speak up for your husband?"

Alicia frowned. "I'm afraid to say they are all . . ."

"I'm the only one left," Gregory stepped up. "Other than Hilary, of course."

"That is most unfortunate," Mr. Collings declared. "But, if that's what we have to work with, I'm sure we will manage."

The barrister's words didn't exactly fill Alicia with confidence. She fought to shake the feeling her husband was on a back footing before he even stood before the judge. Her thoughts spun to the unfortunate Dr. Beauchamp, who'd ended his days soaked in his own filth and begging to be put out of his misery. At least Hilary's demise would be altogether more humane, should it come to that.

"*The Crown versus Hilary St. John*!" the clerk of the court's voice rose above the respectful thrum of voices in the Old Bailey foyer.

"Looks like it's curtain time." Dudley Bartlett's chipper tone sounded woefully out of place. "Let's get this over and done with and your husband back home where he belongs."

It crossed Alicia's mind to remind her father the cottage had been razed to the ground, all but its chimney stack, but decided to let it go—there were far bigger things of concern than being pedantic.

Judge Percy Rawcliffe was one of only twelve full-time judges in the whole of Britain. Known simply and somewhat uncreatively as "The Twelve," each was appointed for life. They had the job of sitting at permanent courts such as the Old Bailey as opposed to the various assize courts that dealt with crimes much less serious than murder, treason, and such. He was a stout fellow with a round, ruddy face, which sported a greying handlebar moustache. Alicia thought it made him look quite grandfatherly and level-headed.

Alicia, Gregory, Dudley, and Mr. Collings sat in silence as the jury filed in to take their place on the twin rows of wooden benches at the left-hand side of the courtroom. The place smelled nicely of scented flowers and herbs which were strategically placed about courtrooms to prevent the spread of disease and mask the stink of unwashed prisoners. Alicia picked out rosemary, thyme, and sage amongst the potpourri of aromas.

With the motley assortment of jurors in place, Judge Rawcliffe had the guards bring Hilary into the court, at which point Alicia feared she might faint.

Her poor, sweet Hilary looked ghastly.

Dressed in filthy, dark-grey prison shirt and trousers, his face was covered with grime, other than along his cheeks where his tears had washed it away. He appeared thin, his features gaunt, and he grimaced with each step as the iron shackles bit into his bare ankles. His eyes met with his wife's across the courtroom, which may as well have been the vast expanse of an ocean, and Alicia saw deep embarrassment there as if her darling husband was more ashamed of his appearance than the predicament he had inadvertently placed them both into.

"Dr. Hilary St. John," the judge began, his voice booming and most pompous, "you are accused of the most heinous of crimes—that of high treason against King George, may God rest his immortal soul, and the Crown. How do you plead?"

One of the pair of mean-looking guards flanking Hilary poked him in the back, which was entirely unnecessary.

"Not guilty." Hilary's voice was barely above a whisper, like that of a dying old man.

"Very well," Judge Rawcliffe said with a heavy sigh, as if he had been hoping that Hilary would have chosen the easier option and he could be on his way to an early lunch. "What say you, Mr. Fortescue?"

The prosecutor, a spry young chap of thirty years or so, all but leapt to his feet. "If I may, your honour, this will take nought but a few minutes—the case against Dr. St. John is cut-and-dried. We will have it all over and done with in time for the ship to Australia."

Alicia had heard trials were apt to be obscenely quick—even those of such a serious matter as Hilary's—and judges often sat through a dozen or so in a single day. Even so, she found the young prosecutor's attitude to be most unseemly. "It's as if they have decided my husband's guilt even before we have begun," she hissed into Mr. Collings's ear.

"I'm afraid that is often the case, my dear," the barrister said. "But I'm sure that will not be so for Dr. St. John."

"Dr. Hilary St. John." Fortescue jabbed a finger in Hilary's direction. "When you worked as one of the king's physicians, you conspired with others to bring harm to him in order to damage the throne so irreparably a foreign power could simply walk in and take command of our great country."

"I did not." Hilary fixed the fellow with an icy stare.

"And you concocted a web of deceit, along with your coconspirators, that would make it look as if you had, indeed, discovered what ailed King George and what may be administered by means of a cure."

"We discovered the King's madness was caused by a simple disorder of the blood," Hilary said. "A disorder we hypothesised could be treated by additional iron within a carefully structured diet."

"And is there a name for this sickness that can be treated by feeding a king *steel*?" The prosecutor made no bones about the fact he was openly mocking Hilary.

"It has no name as yet." Hilary was most firm. "And it's *iron*, which occurs naturally in many foods."

Mr. Collings stood up as quickly as his old bones would allow. The sudden movement startled Alicia, who had been focussed upon her husband.

"I would like to present to the court the actual findings of Dr. St. John, Dr. Alexander Beauchamp, and others," the barrister declared as he placed the sheaf of papers he had pulled from the satchel onto the table before him.

"Mr. Collings!" Judge Rawcliffe blustered. "This is most unprecedented! You are only permitted to advise your client on points of law, or have you forgotten that along with your good manners?"

"I do apologise for my untimely outburst, but I have here the *actual* documentation that proves Dr. St. John had only the king's best interests at heart, and therefore is no guiltier of treason than you or I."

"And is such a cure able to be administered to King George?" The judge peered down at the barrister with a smug look upon his face.

Alicia's heart sank even further than she thought it could ever go. Mr. Collings had impressed her with his burst into action, but she rather feared he was casting grain upon stony ground.

"No, your honour," the barrister replied.

"And why is that pray tell?"

"Because, as the court is well aware, King George passed away two days ago." Mr. Collings sounded somewhat deflated.

"And what is to say Dr. St. John and his nefarious cohorts were not the ones who put paid to our king's life?" Judge Rawcliffe appeared rather delighted with that notion.

"If only Mad King George hadn't kicked the bucket." Dudley whispered loudly in his daughter's ear. "Most inopportune timing, if you ask me."

Her father was correct, if somewhat disrespectful, and Alicia could only look on helplessly as the judge chastised her husband's barrister for his interruption of the proceedings and totally ignored the evidence he was attempting to present to the court. The whole thing had the distinct air of a foregone conclusion, which meant Hilary's fate had been all but sealed before he'd so much as set foot in the Old Bailey.

"Since there is no way we can ascertain if Dr. St. John's diagnosis and supposed 'cure' is genuine," the prosecutor picked up again the moment the berated Mr. Collings had sat himself back down, "then the only plausible verdict has to be *guilty*."

"No!" Alicia couldn't help herself. "This is not fair!" Looking across at the jury, who were busy chatting amongst themselves, she implored, "I beg you to give my husband the right and proper trial he deserves . . . *Please*!"

"Do you need to deliberate?" Judge Rawcliffe asked of the jury's foreman.

"No, your honour." The reply came as no surprise.

"Then, what say you in the case of the Crown versus Dr. Hilary St. John?"

"We find the defendant guilty."

The judge let out what could only have been a loud sigh of relief. "Dr. St. John, whilst I feel obliged to sentence you to hang at Tyburn out of respect for our dearly departed king, I have been instructed that the colonies are in dire need of medical practitioners of your calibre. Therefore, I shall sentence you to be transported to Australia, where you will live out your days as a criminal."

"But, your honour, I have not been permitted to speak," Hilary croaked.

"You have nothing to say that I wish to hear." Judge Rawcliffe slammed down his gavel and addressed the court guards, "Take him down."

Alicia sobbed as Hilary was jostled from the court by the guards. She wanted nothing more than to dash across that drab, horrible room and fling her arms about his neck. How she wanted to kiss his soft, tender lips and feel the warmth of his body next to hers. Instead, all she had by means of consolation was her father's heavy snorting and Gregory's arm surreptitiously draped around her shoulders as they heaved with her crying. Even Edmund was noticeable by his absence—just where was he in her hour of need?

"This can't be it, Josiah," Dudley barked as the court door closed behind Hilary.

"I'm afraid it is, old chap," Mr. Collins told him. "The ship sets sail tonight—it looks like somebody wanted to make sure your son-in-law was on it."

"There *has* to be something we can do," Alicia said through her tears. "There *must* be!"

"Unless you have means by which to facilitate your husband's escape, Mrs. St. John, I'm afraid to say there is absolutely nothing . . ."

Alicia didn't hear anything else the old barrister had to say. Driven by despair at the thought of never seeing her precious Hilary again, the grief-stricken cogs of her inner mind began to turn as Edmund's voice drifted through her thoughts. "If that is to be the case, then it would appear you have only the one option, my dear Alicia," he said. "We must liberate Hilary from prison before he gets on that ship . . ."

Chapter Thirty-One

"The King George IV sets sail this very night," Gregory reminded Alicia as they sat amongst the rich décor of her parents' parlour.

"What an unfortunate name for a transportation ship, given the current state of affairs," Alicia replied with a wry smile. She had not managed her afternoon nap following Hilary's appalling day in court, and her brain was a tad foggy.

"They have hastily renamed many ships in honour of our new king," Gregory explained. "I believe Hilary's was known as The Retribution when it docked a week ago."

"Please don't refer to it as my husband's ship," Alicia beseeched. "I really do hate the very thought of him setting foot on that dreadful vessel because I know, should he do so, it will be the very last I see of him."

Leaning forward, Gregory reached out a hand as if to place it upon Alicia's knee. At the last moment, he clearly decided against such action—most likely because Dorothea was bustling around in that part of the house—and the hand was retracted. "Do remember the conversation we had in York, my dear," he said. "My offer still stands . . . should the unthinkable happen."

"Thank you, Gregory," Alicia said with nary a smile. "That is most kind of you. However, I am not prepared to think the unthinkable just yet, not when there is a chance—"

"A *slim* chance." She may have imagined it, but Alicia would have sworn she detected just a touch of glee in Gregory's tone as he corrected her.

"A slim chance is still a chance nonetheless," Alicia insisted. "Do tell me what other information you have managed to glean regarding the King George IV."

"Well . . ." Gregory leaned back in the high-backed chair and crossed his legs like a proper gentleman. "I understand from my sources that prisoners sentenced to deportation are transported from the various gaols—Newgate, Fleet, the Tower, of course—and escorted onto the prison hulk moored close to Woolwich Arsenal."

"You are well-versed, Gregory," Alicia was impressed. "How does one come to know such information and people who are apt to divulge it?"

"It is best you do not ask me that," Gregory replied with a thin smile. He stroked at his beard as if deep in thought. "Suffice it to say, with living in Whitechapel, I have come to know many men of somewhat dubious character. It is not becoming of a gentlewoman of your standing to ask such a question."

"Forgive me," Alicia took her admonishment well. "Do go on . . ."

"The prisoners will all be in chains, of course—I do believe they actually chain them together, which makes escape all but impossible. But . . . there is a brief period during which they leave the prison carriages and make their way to the ship that they are unshackled. My understanding is the guards do it just in case one of the rapscallions decides to end his misery in the Thames—it just wouldn't do for him to take all of his fellow inmates with him."

"Is it possible to make good an escape that way?" Alicia's mind was finally beginning to stir into action and frantically searched for opportunities. "Hilary is quite the strong swimmer."

Gregory shook his head. "Men have tried, naturally. I'm sorry to say, at this time of the year, the water will be so freezing cold it could stop a chap's heart the instant he submerged. And even if it did not, it would suck the very life from him before he swam more than a few yards. That's supposing he wasn't crushed between the side of the ship and the dock, of course."

"That all sounds ghastly." Alicia's mind was tortured by thoughts of her husband meeting with that terrible fate, his body squashed by the huge wooden bough of the transportation ship.

"And, even if he were to survive *that*, the Thames water is filthy with human waste from across the city, and likely riddled with cholera. Poor Hilary really wouldn't stand a chance."

Memories of Edmund's undignified demise courtesy of that terrible sickness flooded Alicia's head. To lose her husband in the same way really would be far too much for her to bear. The more Gregory spoke, the more futile their plan sounded. "So, what are we to do, Gregory?"

"We can bribe one of the prison guards to turn a blind eye shortly after the prisoners are unshackled and leave the carriages. The short walk across the dock will give Hilary the chance to run—if, indeed, he is still capable of doing so."

"Gregory!" Alicia snapped. "Why would you say such a horrible thing?"

"I'm so sorry, Alicia. It is simply my clumsy way of preparing you for the worst. Prison guards can be a thoroughly unpleasant lot, and I've heard they take their pleasure tormenting and torturing their charges, especially those incarcerated for treason."

"Oh, dear Lord, no." Alicia clasped her hands tight in her lap and concentrated upon keeping her tears at bay.

"I am positive Hilary will be perfectly capable, though." Gregory looked a tad embarrassed as he backtracked. "Why, he seemed in fine fettle at the Old Bailey earlier—despite everything."

"Then let's assume he will be in the same condition this evening."

"Agreed." Gregory sat forward in his chair again; this time there was no outstretched hand.

"How easy will it be to bribe a prison guard?" Alicia asked. It truly was a question she never thought she would hear passing her own lips.

"They are paid a meagre wage and have a passion for the gin houses and women of loose morals abundant about the docklands." Gregory spoke as if selecting each word carefully so as not to offend Alicia's sensibilities. "I have spoken to my source, and he assured me it is as good as done. Just as soon as he discovers which of the Tower guards will be escorting your husband, the bribe will be made."

"And this source of yours? Can he be trusted?"

Gregory let out a light, squeaking laugh that was most unbecoming of a gentleman. "He is a fellow who bribes the king's guards, what do you think?"

"Then, are we not incredibly foolish to base our entire plan upon his supposed actions?"

"That is not something you ought to be worrying about, my dear," Gregory did his best to reassure. "You need to be thinking about where you and your husband will go once he is a free man. You certainly cannot return here, or to Spitalfields. Hilary will be a fugitive from the law, and the authorities will stop at nothing to find him."

"All we will require is enough time to clear his name, Gregory." Alicia was most determined on that subject. "And once we do so, he will be afforded a full pardon, and we shall resume our lives."

"I sincerely hope that to be the case, Alicia," Gregory replied with a wise nod of the head. "Now, we must concentrate upon the matter at hand—we really do not have too much time at all. Tell me, will your brother be joining us on our adventure?"

Alicia shook her head. "I have not told Oliver of our plans at all," she said. "Were things to go terribly awry, I would hate for him to end up alongside us in the Tower. For one, Mother and Father would never forgive me."

Gregory seemed relieved to hear that news. "Then, we have only ourselves to think about, which is most preferable—too many cooks spoil the broth and so forth."

"So . . ." Alicia prompted. "What do we do when the guard turns that blind eye of his?"

Chapter Thirty-Two

The night held within its darkness a particular kind of damp that gave aching bones to even the hardiest of individuals and had Alicia longing for the warmth of a crackling log fire. Along with that, the pungent stink of human waste wafting in from the Thames did little to ease the queasy feeling she had in the pit of her stomach, although that had more to do with what the evening held in store than the smell.

"We must remain out of sight until the prison carriages arrive," Gregory stated the blindingly obvious. "We can't afford to be seen." He crouched down alongside Alicia behind a piled-high stack of crates, one of a multitude by the side of the expansive dockside warehouse.

The dock itself was all but deserted other than the occasional crew members boarding and alighting the erstwhile named Retribution. The prison hulk was making ready to take Hilary thousands of miles away to Australia. Not one of them so much as glanced in the direction of the two secretive figures lurking about the dock, and Alicia reckoned they'd be too wrapped up in their own business to be peering into the shadows.

"Did you *have* to bring that along?" Alicia pointed at the flintlock pistol protruding rather conspicuously from the waistband of his breeches. She recognised it as a double-barrel Gribeauval—Father had brought one home from a trip to France, and Mother abhorred the thing. "You know how I despise firearms."

"I shall only use it if entirely necessary," Gregory told her. "And if it makes the difference between us being caught and finding ourselves upon that rather unpleasant boat, I have a feeling you will feel differently."

"Perhaps that's the answer," Alicia mused. "I may be looking at this situation in the wrong way. Maybe instead of preventing Hilary from boarding, we should be planning on helping me stowaway *with* him."

"Don't be so ridiculous!" Gregory hissed. His tone was somewhat sharper than Alicia cared for. "You couldn't possibly stay concealed for the entire trip, and how do you think you would fare as the only woman aboard a ship filled to the gunnels with men—all criminals and vagabonds, to boot?!"

"I'm sure Hilary would protect me," Alicia replied.

"And how would he possibly manage that against almost five hundred desperate men?" Gregory replied. "He may be a strong man with right on his side, but not even Hilary St. John is *that* powerful."

"He's right, Alicia," Edmund's voice floated into her mind. "You must clear your head of any fanciful thoughts of that nature. Your only hope is to ensure Hilary does *not* get onto that ship."

"I know, I know," Alicia said, not realising she was speaking out loud. "Can't a woman have a flight of fancy anymore?"

"This is hardly the time for frippery, Alicia," Gregory said. His voice startled Alicia, as she'd been expecting the response to come from Edmund. How terribly confusing the whole situation with Edmund's ghost was becoming. Alicia was beginning to lose track of what she was saying, and to whom.

"Once again, your husband's friend is correct," Edmund told her. "I know he can be abrasive, but it would certainly behove you to follow his direction—you would not survive above a week on board that prison hulk."

"I promise I will, Edmund." Alicia was sure to give the reply inside her head. She didn't wish for Gregory to think she was losing her nerve and talking to imaginary people.

The rhythmic sound of horses' hooves resounded along the dockside, bouncing from the soot-stained brick walls of the warehouses and out across the cold, still river. A little way along the dock, three long, black carriages appeared—each one with thick iron bars over its windows.

"How do we know Hilary is in one of those?" Alicia whispered in Gregory's ear as they both hunkered down still further behind the sanctuary of their crate pile. It was a valid question for, if her understanding was correct, those three carriages were the first of many that would deposit their cargo of hapless deportees throughout the night.

"I just know," Gregory replied with an annoyed hiss. "I have it on good authority they always bring prisoners from the Tower first—it's kind of a privilege of rank thing."

Alicia couldn't for the life of her imagine how being first onto that hideous ship could ever be considered a privilege, but somehow it did make some kind of warped sense. What really mattered was she was about to be reunited with her beloved husband—providing all went according to plan and Gregory's bribery worked as it was supposed to.

The first batch of prisoners clambered from the leading carriage, followed by the second lot from the one behind.

"I can't see Hilary at all," Alicia said quietly. She tried to ignore the sinking feeling gnawing away deep down in her gut.

"Have patience!" Gregory replied with an annoyed grunt. "And do be quiet!"

Alicia clamped her lips tight shut and looked the best she could through the gloom, her eyes searching the desolate face of each prisoner walking single file towards the ship. They passed beneath the flickering gaslights along the way, which illuminated their route with an eerie yellow glow.

And there he was.

Her dearest, darling husband, Hilary.

"Excellent," Gregory murmured beneath his breath. "They put him last on the chain."

Hilary was, indeed, the very last man out from the third carriage. He was chained at the end of the line of a dozen prisoners, all clad in the same grey garb. As Alicia watched—fighting the urge to dash across the dock and hold him tight—the men were all lined up in a single row whilst one of the guards began unlocking the shackles that rattled about their hands and feet. The chains were forged from heavy iron, and Alicia could see just how easily they would drag the prisoners down to the muddy bed of the Thames in an instant.

Suddenly, Gregory was no longer by her side.

Looking around, Alicia espied him making his way towards the prisoners, using the crates as cover. He stooped low as he walked, presumably to offer as little of himself as possible to the scrutiny of the prison officers.

He really needn't have bothered.

The guards, of which there were a half dozen—two from each of the carriages—were armed with swords and pistols and seemed more intent on making lewd conversation between themselves than being aware of their surroundings. Alicia guessed that was why they chose to transport the prisoners to the ship under cover of the night—nobody in their right mind would be skulking about the docks at that hour and in such foul weather. The guard with the keys, which were looped onto a huge, iron ring, worked diligently at unfastening the prisoners under the sparse light offered by the nearby lamps.

Following Gregory, Alicia kept her head low, too, and before long they had made it to less than twenty yards from the prisoners and their armed guardians without detection.

Once each of the three-dozen prisoners were unshackled, the guards had them move forwards in single file to where the prison hulk's precarious-looking gangplank awaited. To a man, they followed the guards' instructions with a slow, shuffling walk and expressionless faces. It was as if they had been broken by their time in prison, made complicit by the erosion of their very humanity.

Alicia's heart went out to each one of them. No matter what crime they had committed to bring them to such a dreadful juncture in their lives, she truly believed no man deserved to be so cruelly broken as to accept their fate with nary a glimmer of defiance. Perhaps, she thought, for many of the destroyed souls out there on the dockside, the hangman's noose would have been the more humane punishment.

Hilary walked a tad slower than his fellow inmates, dragging his feet along the cold, dank bricks of the dock, and in no time at all, there was a sizeable gap between him and the last man in that depressing line.

The guard bringing up the rear seemed not to notice. In fact, Alicia watched with astonishment as he upped his own step and walked straight by Hilary. Evidently, he was the one who had so gladly taken Gregory's bribe. And, as the guard did so, he began whistling some dry, tuneless tune Alicia had no chance of identifying.

That was the signal.

Chapter Thirty-Three

Gregory dashed out from the concealing shadows of the myriad crates and, before anyone could so much as register what was going on, he had punched the guard to the ground.

"*Gregory*?" Hilary's lips barely moved as he mumbled his surprise.

Alicia saw the puzzlement in her husband's eyes as he watched Gregory drag the unconscious guard away from the line of prisoners and into the gloomy sanctuary amongst the empty crates.

The guard made no sound as Gregory lay him down against the crates near Alicia. She had no doubt the pantomime of being knocked to the ground had been all part of the act—albeit a brutally realistic one—just in case one of the guard's colleagues happened to see anything. Perhaps Gregory had neither the means nor the influence to bribe all of them.

"What's going on?" Hilary demanded of his friend.

"*Shh*!" Gregory pressed a finger to Hilary's lips. His eyes darted across to the prisoners, the first of whom was already boarding the ship. Slowly, he lowered his finger—the prisoners and guards were out of earshot.

"Hilary?" Alicia stepped out from her hiding place.

"Alicia?" Tears welled in Hilary's eyes as he saw his wife make her way towards him from the darkness.

Alicia dashed the remaining few yards and flung herself into Hilary's arms—not caring that such a display of affection in front of Gregory may embarrass her husband. Hilary was of the same mind, too, and lifted her up in a strong embrace, his powerful arms holding her tight and sweeping her up off the ground all at the same time.

Casting caution still further to the wind, Alicia planted a long, lingering kiss upon her husband's lips, savouring the warmth and taste of him—it felt to her like they had been apart a hundred years or more, and finally he was home. Only, they were a long way from home, and Hilary was not only a convicted traitor but also an escaped prisoner and fugitive to boot. Despite the euphoria of once more being in the arms of her beloved, Alicia knew all too well they were not out of the woods by a long chalk.

"Very touching indeed." Gregory's voice sounded low and gravelly in the gloom.

Concerned her unseemly show of affection towards Hilary had offended Gregory in some way, Alicia extricated herself from the warmth of her husband's body and wonderfully strong arms. "Do forgive me, Gregory," she said, "it has been quite some time . . ."

Gregory was pointing his pistol directly at her, his eyes narrowed and glinting as he stepped out from the shadows.

"Steady on, old chap!" Acting upon instinct, Hilary manoeuvred himself in front of Alicia and held out a hand, as if that would stop a lead ball.

Gregory shrugged. "That won't help either of you," he growled. "I don't much care who I shoot first."

"I should have known!" Edmund's voice bounded into Alicia's mind as she stared with profound disbelief at Gregory and the fearsome gun he was aiming squarely at Hilary's broad chest. Her dead fiancé seemed intensely vexed with himself. "I *knew* your nemesis was drawing close, but I had no inkling he had been close by all along!"

Alicia tuned Edmund out; her primary instinct was to get out of this peculiar turn of events with her and Hilary intact, and she did not need the distraction. That her ghostly fiancé had not been able to see into this particular part of the future was no longer here nor there.

"Is this because I refused to entertain the notion of being with you?" Alicia had to ask. Eyeing the twin barrels of Gregory's gun, they put her in mind of the malevolent eyes of some evil, otherworldly devil, a bringer of death.

"He did *what*?" Hilary bristled. "Gregory, you absolute . . . *cad*!"

Gregory laughed and took a step closer. "You flatter yourself, Mrs. St John." There was a distinct bluntness to the formality that suggested detachment on Gregory's part; he really did mean to kill Alicia and Hilary. "This is all far bigger than a mere woman could even begin to imagine. This is about the crown and the future of England—it always has been."

"You are part of the plot to topple King George?" Hilary was quite incredulous at the notion.

Gregory nodded. "And it all comes from within the palace walls, my esteemed friend," he said with a knowing smirk. "Have either of you stopped to question why it is I was the only one of the king's physicians working on the supposed cure who was neither dead nor imprisoned?"

"I trusted you, Gregory," Hilary spat.

"As did I." Alicia was beyond angry with herself. How on earth did she not see the wretched man for who—and what—he truly was?! She had allowed herself to be drawn in by his faux sympathy and helpfulness, and she felt like a proper fool indeed.

"All of which made my job much easier than it could have been." Gregory alternated the pistol's aim between both of his targets. "And good King George kicking the old bucket when he did has made *everything* easy now. I was beginning to think I might have to kill the mad old fool myself."

"You wouldn't dare!" Hilary was rightly outraged at his fellow doctor's treacherous talk.

"Wouldn't I?" Gregory smiled. "Although to kill the king outright would have brought with it many dangers, not least of all to the crown itself."

"You'd have been hung on the spot!" Alicia growled.

"Yes, that's certainly *one* of the dangers." Gregory laughed at that idea as if he was finding the whole affair exceptionally amusing. "Which was why I had to ensure your work was entirely discredited,

Dr. St. John—along with your good self, of course. Nobody would ever have believed a traitor, nor allow him anywhere near the king to try out the alleged miracle cure. At that point, you were worth more alive and branded a traitor than dead like the others, my dear friend."

"You murdered Dr. Beauchamp!" Alicia joined up the dots.

"I merely administered a little arsenic to the fool's beer," Gregory told her. "Once the whereabouts of his papers were known to me, he was of no further use. I also made sure none of the good folk of York with whom he had dealings were left in any position to speak to the authorities—the haberdasher, the young man at the gun shop, and that awful blabbermouth at the tavern. I must say, I was perfectly exhausted following our northern excursion, my dear Alicia." That wicked smile again. "I did thoroughly enjoy your company, though—I was pleased the fire didn't put you off as I'd originally intended."

"Fire?" Hilary demanded. "What fire?"

"The cottage." Alicia hated to have to tell him his beloved cottage was gone, especially like that. "It burned down the night after you were taken away—and now we know by whom." She nodded towards Gregory, who appeared unmoved by the revelation.

"You absolute scoundrel." Hilary took a step forward, fists clenched.

"Stay where you are, Hilary." Gregory wiggled the pistol to emphasise his intentions. "There really is little point in you playing the hero. The moment your fellow prisoners and their guards are on the ship, it'll be time for we three to say our final goodbyes.

"Why all this charade, Gregory?" Alicia spoke up. "Why not just allow Hilary to be deported and be done with your perfidy?"

"That was always the plan." Gregory kept the gun steady, aimed directly between Hilary's eyes. "Although a one-way trip to Tyburn's gallows would have been a more preferable outcome, as it happens. With the king dead, it was better Hilary not live to tell any tales—there's always the chance someone may pay attention to the ramblings of a discredited doctor, even in the Antipodes."

"You planned to make all this appear like I was killed making my final bid for freedom?" Hilary interjected.

A nod from Gregory. "And I think, deep, deep down in here—" He placed his free hand over his heart. "I harboured a little hope that if Alicia were to see me as the hero who attempted to free you, she would fall in love with me."

"I would never fall in love with a despicable creature like you, Gregory Sedgewick—*never*!" Alicia felt sick to her stomach at the very thought.

"Ah well," Gregory sighed. "In which case, I suppose this is all for the best, then."

So saying, he cocked the flintlock and took aim.

Chapter Thirty-Four

In the blink of an eye, Hilary darted forwards, his body shielding Alicia, and made a grab for Gregory's pistol.

Startled, Gregory stepped back a pace or two before discharging the flintlock. The heavy weapon bucked in his hand like some wild animal, and the sharp crack of the gunshot split the cold night air.

"*Hilary*!" Alicia's scream was shrill, and she had no care her voice could be heard all the way across to the boat. Distraught, she looked on helplessly as her husband clutched at his chest and crumpled to the ground writhing in pain and groaning with a wet, gurgling sound.

In the fragmented moment that seemed an eternity, Gregory stared down at his would-be friend with an expression akin to surprise. Was it possible he had not truly meant to shoot Hilary, or was it simply a matter of him having not expected the pistol to fire when it did?

Not wishing to find out, whilst Gregory made to cock the flintlock's second hammer, Alicia ran at him with her fists balled tight. She had picked up some choice pugilistic moves from her wayward brother, and now was as good a time as any to put them into practice.

Gregory's head snapped back as Alicia caught him with a determined haymaker square on the chin. Staggering backwards, he pinwheeled his one free arm in a desperate attempt to maintain his balance, all the while clutching onto his uncocked pistol.

Alicia lay another punch, followed by another, upon Gregory's face, the roughness of his beard chaffing her bare knuckles. Oliver had taught her the importance of not relying upon just one strike and to keep on going until the opponent was on the ground and senseless.

"*Stop it*!" Gregory whined as the skin below his left eye split and a thin trickle of blood coloured his cheek. He lifted both arms to defend his face from Alicia's onslaught, yet steadfastly refused to let go of the pistol.

Another flurry of punches had Gregory pressed up against a teetering stack of crates. Alicia's fists were mostly hitting the blaggard's arms, but she definitely had him on the back footing. All the while, her thoughts were with Hilary, and she prayed she could save him, if not herself.

In her fury and desperation to put Gregory on the ground where he could do no more harm, Alicia forgot one of Oliver's golden rules of boxing: an animal cornered is the most dangerous of all . . .

With a resolute, angry snarl, Gregory swung the pistol down at Alicia. Seeing the sudden moment, she ducked her head, but alas, she was a fragment of a second too late. The hard metal of the flintlock caught her a sharp, glancing blow on the temple.

Dazed, Alicia fought to stay on her feet. The warm sensation of blood running down the side of her face spurred her on—to fall down now would likely mean the end of both herself and Hilary. A savage blow to the solar plexus forced the air from Alicia's stomach and had her involuntarily bending over. The cornered animal that was Gregory Sedgewick was evidently not above hitting women, which made him more of a cad in Alicia's eyes.

"Now, will you do the decent thing and die, you infernal harpy!?" Gregory growled, and Alicia heard the distinctive *click* of the pistol.

Struggling to draw breath, heart thumping, Alicia straightened herself up to confront the wicked man. "*Never*!" she yelled in his face and brought up her knee sharply into Gregory's nether regions.

Oliver would have been ashamed of his sister for such an illegal move—whilst it did happen on occasion in some of the dirtier boxing matches, a knee to the groin was most definitely against the London Prize Ring Rules!

"*Harridan*!" Gregory groaned as he took his turn to bend double and, as both hands instinctively shot downwards to protect his injured area, the pistol slipped from his fingers and fell to the ground.

Seizing her chance, yet still gasping for breath, Alicia snatched up the flintlock that lay quite impotently at Gregory's feet. Although she had never fired a gun in her life, and had never had any intention of doing so, she reckoned she could at least use the horrible thing to keep Gregory at bay whilst she summoned help. She was surprised that her scream and the first gunshot had not brought any of the gaol guards or crew running from the ship.

"You need to stay where you are, Gregory," Alicia told her nemesis as she took a step or two away from him with the flintlock aimed between his evil little eyes. "I promise I *will* shoot you on the spot if you dare move."

Straightening up with a pained expression screwing up his thin face, Gregory glowered at her. He reached out one hand, keeping the other between his legs in a most vulgar manner, as if concerned the contents of his breeches would spill out onto the dock should he remove it. "Give me the pistol, Alicia." Gregory's words dripped with menace. "I promise I'll make your deaths quick and painless." He glanced over at where Hilary lay on the ground. He was still holding onto his chest, his prison-issued shirt wet with blood, but he was barely moving.

"You are a wicked man, Gregory," Alicia admonished. "But I do not believe you are so foolish as to expect I shall simply hand over the implement of my own demise." The slightest of laughs tripped off Alicia's tongue at the absurdity of it all.

"Do you honestly think I am the end of this?" Gregory taunted her. "Even if you were to finish me off tonight, there are others who will seek to silence that interfering, puritanical husband of yours—and you too, my dear Alicia. The conspiracy to destroy the throne runs deep into England's high society, and there is certainly no shortage of gentlemen who will stop at nothing to see their plans come to fruition."

"You don't frighten me, Gregory Sedgewick," Alicia wiggled the pistol.

"You are a feisty one for sure, Mrs. St. John, but you would be well-advised to be afraid," Gregory said with a weasel-thin smile. "Sooner or later, you and Hilary will meet your maker—another mysterious fire perhaps or maybe even a lead ball for both you and your husband when you least expect it. What say you hand over that pistol and go peacefully at the hand of a friend?"

"You are no friend of mine!" Alicia spat. For a split second, she actually contemplated squeezing the trigger to put an end to the wretched man she had trusted so completely. She would certainly learn to trust her initial gut feeling towards people in the future!

If, indeed, she had a future.

That moment's hesitation was all Gregory needed.

Leaping forward with all the agility of a feral alley cat, he grasped the wrist of the hand holding the flintlock with one hand and wrapped the strong, spindly fingers of the other about Alicia's throat. The momentum carried them both a couple of yards across the dock before Alicia lost her footing and tumbled backwards.

As she fell, Alicia felt something crack inside, which she presumed to be a rib or two since the sound—much akin to wet, green twigs snapping underfoot—was accompanied by a sharp pain that reached out to every corner of her body with fiery tendrils of pain. It felt so terribly wrong to find herself beneath Gregory Sedgewick in such a way, and the genteel lady within her simply screamed out at the indecency of it all. However, it was the least of Alicia's worries as Gregory crushed her windpipe with grim determination and twisted at her wrist in order to wrest the pistol from her grasp.

"Shoot him, Alicia!" Edmund's voice poked through the greyness that was already beginning to creep around the edges of her consciousness. "Point the muzzle at his nasty little face and pull that trigger!"

"*Don't you think I would if I could?*" Alicia replied with her thoughts as she struggled beneath Gregory's weight. Sometimes Edmund's attempts at being helpful could be intensely irritating, even though they were meant with the best of intentions. "*The man has my arm pinned and he is far stronger than he looks!*"

At that moment, a stabbing pain shot through Alicia's arm and her fingers sprang open, releasing the pistol. Gregory had snapped the fragile bones of her wrist.

Alicia cried out as the agony spread all the way along her arm. Gregory seized the flintlock and climbed off her.

At least, with Gregory's hand no longer constricting her neck, Alicia was able to breathe—the question was: for how much longer?

"Right, where were we?" Gregory smiled down at Alicia like the head of the hunt contemplating a wounded fox before setting the hounds about their final task. The man she'd considered a true friend seemed to be delighting in the reversal of fortune, savouring the deadly moment.

Alicia found herself once again staring down the twin barrels of Gregory's Gribeauval and praying for some kind of miracle—this time she was laid prone upon the damp ground and clearly at the disadvantage.

From the corner of her eye, Alicia saw a movement. At first, she thought it was one of the guards and her heart filled with hope. But no, it was a nebulous, floating shape drifting away from her and in the direction of the guard Gregory had knocked unconscious.

Edmund.

The ghostly shape, which was unmistakably that of her dead fiancé, hovered over the guard a moment or two before settling into the man's recumbent body, as one might an exceptionally comfy chaise lounge.

And then, as Alicia watched in the periphery of her vision, the guard struggled to his feet and began to make his way towards her. The man's gait was uneven and comically wobbly, which put Alicia in mind of a newborn calf finding its feet for the very first time. His rugged face wore the blank expression of one who might simply be sleepwalking.

"You don't have to do this, Gregory." Alicia decided it best to engage the man to buy as much time as possible for Edmund to execute his daring plan. Just how on earth he'd managed to take control of the guard's body in such a manner was beyond her comprehension, although she had an idea it was surely akin to witchcraft!

"I truly am so very sorry, my dear Alicia," Gregory said from behind the fearsome pistol. "There really is no other way."

A sudden movement to his left caught Gregory's attention. With a barely imperceptible flick of his head, he glanced over in the direction of the approaching guard. "What the . . .?"

The guard, manoeuvred from within by Edmund, slipped behind a high stack of crates and out of Gregory's line of sight. He had given away his element of surprise and alerted Gregory—there was simply too much distance between them for him to make a grab for the gun.

"Looks like I'll have to finish this right now, Alicia." Gregory sounded terribly matter of fact. Taking a step closer, he aimed the pistol at Alicia's head, using the drying blood there as a makeshift target. "I really do wish things had turned out differently," he said. "I honestly believe I could have made you so very happy."

Fearing the inevitable, Alicia stared with unerring defiance at Gregory. If he was to put an end to her life, then he was going to jolly well have to look into her eyes as he did so.

There came a low creaking sound, and another movement distracted Gregory from his nefarious intentions; this time, a stack of crates toppled down towards him.

Gregory let out a yelp and lifted his arms to protect his head from the falling crates as they crashed on top of him, raining hard, wooden blows to render him quite helpless. Gregory sank to his knees as a second pile of crates fell upon him, each one battering his body and head as resolutely as Alicia had done mere moments before.

Alicia rolled away from the descending crates in a most unladylike manner, only just missing having her own body pummelled by the cascade of wood Edmund had brought down upon her would-be assassin. She curled herself into a protective ball and prayed the crates would miss her.

After what felt like an eternity filled with crashing, splintering wood, and Gregory's cries of pain, silence once more blanketed the dockside.

"You can get up now, Alicia," said an unfamiliar voice. "You are quite safe."

Alicia unfurled herself like a hedgehog emerging from its winter's sleep to see the guard standing over her, his face blank and expressionless. In his hand was Gregory's pistol. Alicia feared she was not quite as safe as the strange voice had promised, even though Gregory lay half-buried beneath the myriad crates, his body still.

"It's me, Alicia." The guard spoke quietly, as if struggling to form even those three simple words.

"Edmund?" Alicia got to her feet and brushed herself down—her outer coat was somewhat ruined by the muck and grime of the dockyard. "How . . .?"

"It would appear I can do this." The guard spread his arms wide, and some semblance of a smile curled up the corners of his mouth. "I only wish I'd known sooner, my darling Alicia."

Alicia fell into Edmund's arms and held him tight—she was not so foolish as to forget she was actually hugging the prison guard, but in her heart, Alicia *felt* Edmund's spirit dwelling within and, as the years melted away, she was back with him upon the banks of Sweetheart's Lake.

Alas, it was to be short-lived.

"Oh my goodness!" Alicia broke away from the moment as a stark realisation hit her. "Hilary!"

"He will be as right as ninepence, I promise," Edmund reassured as Alicia raced to her husband's side. Kneeling down beside Hilary, Alicia scooped him up in her arms and was relieved to see his eyes flicker open. A weak smile crossed his handsome lips.

"I hope you are right, my dear Edmund—I couldn't even begin to imagine life without him."

As Edmund nodded the guard's head, his shoulders slumped with fatigue. "You seem to forget I know the future," he said.

"*Some* of it," Alicia corrected with a sideways glance over at Gregory, who was beginning to stir.

Edmund sat himself down upon the ground adjacent to Alicia, as if standing up in the guard's body was becoming altogether too much effort. "Yes, I was unable to see enough in order to warn you of that rapscallion's treachery . . ." Edmund said sadly.

Voices drifted over from the direction of the ship. Looking up from her beloved husband, Alicia saw a trio of heavily built gaol guards walking briskly their way. It appeared that the cacophony she and Gregory had created had attracted some attention.

"You will be safe now, my darling Alicia," Edmund said, his voice weak. "I have truly exhausted myself with all of this, and now I must return to whence I came."

Alicia's tears flowed freely as with a choked voice she asked, "Sweetheart's Lake?" There was hope in Alicia's heart, were that to be the case, she would see him again.

Edmund shook the guard's head sadly. "Heaven," he told her. "I couldn't leave this earth until I knew that you were going to be all right. But now, my work here is done—now it is my time to leave you to be with the man you are meant to be with, Alicia. Enjoy your life together, cherish the many children you will share together, and do great things for the world."

"Thank you, Edmund." Hilary's voice was but a feeble croak. He lifted his head from Alicia's lap to look the guard directly in the eye. "I owe you my life, and that of my wonderful Alicia." With a grunt of pained exertion, Hilary outstretched his arm, offering a hand for the shaking.

"I want everything that is good in this world for both you and Alicia. It is my greatest desire that you both to have a long and happy life together," Edmund said as he reciprocated the firm handshake. "You can thank me by loving Alicia until the day you die, Hilary."

"Indubitably, old chap," Hilary replied with a warm-hearted smile.

The gaol guards were all but upon them, and Alicia began to panic. Surely they would recapture Hilary and cart him off to the dreadful ship and a fate worse than death?

"I must go now." Edmund let go of Hilary's hand and embraced Alicia one final time. "You have a friend in me forever, Alicia. It will be a long wait for me, but I will see you again when you too go through the doors of death. But until then you have a life and a happy life to live with Hilary."

He then, very gently, lay the guard's body down. "One last job to do . . ."

As Alicia and Hilary looked on, the nebulous, ephemeral shape of Edmund Pembroke oozed out of the guard's body and made its silent way over to where Gregory scrabbled his way out from beneath the fallen crates.

Chapter Thirty-Five

Alicia and Hilary walked arm in arm around Sweetheart's Lake. It was the first time she had brought him to her favourite corner of London. With Edmund at rest, Alicia had finally considered it to be appropriate. It was a cold, drab March Sunday afternoon, but Alicia didn't mind that at all—she had her darling husband, who was nicely on the mend from the wound to his chest and so very much in love with her.

They had watched Gregory being hauled off the dockside by the gaol guards and onto the awaiting prison hulk. It had struck neither Alicia nor Hilary as unusual the young doctor who had wreaked so much death and destruction, and who had planned to murder them both, had boarded the King George IV without so much as a single word of protest.

In fact, he'd admitted to the guards he was Hilary St. John, and declared he deserved to be aboard the ship forthwith!

And, for their part, the three guards hadn't questioned the fact he wasn't wearing prison garb, or that his countenance was peculiarly blank and expressionless, his voice monotone—almost as if something altogether foreign was operating him from within.

Edmund had left Gregory's body the moment he was securely shackled in the hold of that cruel, most unpleasant ship, and made his way up to heaven. He chose not to stick around to witness Gregory Sedgewick kicking up an unholy ruckus once he regained his senses and realised where he was. He would no doubt profess his innocence like the huge coward he truly was.

And that had been the end of the matter. By the time Hilary had straightened everything out with the authorities and cleared his name, poor, perfidious Gregory was well on his way to the other side of the globe. The new king had little inkling of the plot to ruin the throne, and the British monarchy was once again safe—at least for the time being.

Life quickly returned to normal for the St. Johns, albeit they were forced to reside with Hilary's parents whilst their cottage was rebuilt from the floorboards up.

"I was thinking maybe we ought to consider York," Alicia said to her husband as they strolled by young couples in love and gaggles of persistent, quacking ducks.

Hilary was somewhat taken aback by the revelation. "You'd *choose* to live up north? What on earth would Dudley and Dorothea have to say about such a notion?"

"It's hardly Africa, my love." Alicia laughed.

"Or Australia, for that matter," Hilary added with a sardonic smile that had Alicia wondering just how Gregory was getting on with his long, arduous voyage.

"It's a nice place, and there's the marvellous Yorkshire countryside, too." Alicia gave Hilary's arm a squeeze. "I'm sure they would welcome a great London doctor with open arms—especially one who was a physician to King George. It will also be quite the perfect place to bring our first child into the world."

Hilary stopped dead in his tracks. "You mean . . .?"

Alicia nodded. "And I think we ought to name him Edmund," she declared.

"*If* it's a boy." A huge, boyish grin spread across Hilary's face.

"Oh, he's a boy, all right," Alicia told her husband with confidence. "I have that on good authority."

Oblivious to the courting couples and associated chaperones milling about them, Alicia and Hilary shared a kiss. Behind them, the murky waters of Sweetheart's Lake sparkled in the chill winter sunshine.

Other books by Sean Kikkert

The Highwayman's Confession

Dark Past

Night of the Wolf

The Trek

Home Evenings for Families

Stronger

Last Days

About the Author

Sean Kikkert was born in Adelaide, South Australia. He spent the early part of his childhood in the Netherlands before returning to Australia.

As a teenager, Sean loved to stay up late reading thrillers. He was spellbound by the questions that came up on every page and the plot twists that added exciting unpredictability, and found these books incredibly hard to put down.

Sean's first job after becoming a lawyer brought him and his family to Canberra, Australia's capital city, where he runs his own law practice, but once the working day is over, Sean writes books to keep people up at night, just as he was kept up late all those years ago.

Sean's published works include *The Highwayman's Confession*, *Dark Past*, *Last Days*, *Stronger*, *Home Evenings for Families*, *Night of the Wolf*, *The Trek*, and *Sweetheart's Lake*.

Learn more about Sean and his books by visiting
www.seankikkert.com

Scan to visit

www.seankikkert.com